P9-DHG-885

STAR WARS

BOOK ONE

THE GLOVE OF DARTH VADER
THE LOST CITY OF THE JEDI
ZORBA THE HUTT'S REVENGE

PAUL DAVIDS
AND HOLLACE DAVIDS

BARNES
&NOBLE
BOOKS
NEW YORK

ACKNOWLEDGMENTS

With thanks to George Lucas, the creator of Star Wars, to Lucy Wilson for her devoted guidance, to Charles Kochman for his unfailing insight, and to West End Games for their wonderful Star Wars sourcebooks—also to Betsy Gould, Judy Gitenstein, Peter Miller, and Richard A. Rosen for their advice and help.

Originally published as three separate volumes

The Glove of Darth Vader
by Paul Davids and Hollace Davids
Copyright © 1992 by LucasFilm, Ltd.

The Lost City of the Jedi
by Paul Davids and Hollace Davids
Copyright © 1992 by LucasFilm, Ltd.

Zorba the Hutt's Revenge
by Paul Davids and Hollace Davids
Copyright © 1992 by LucasFilm, Ltd.

Star Wars is a registered trademark of LucasFilm, Ltd.
All rights reserved. Used under authorization.

This edition published by Barnes & Noble, Inc., by arrangement with Bantam Doubleday Dell Books For Young Readers, a division of Bantam Doubleday Dell Publishing Group, Inc., New York, New York, U.S.A.

All rights reserved. No part of this book may be used or reproduced in any manner whatsoever without the written permission of the Publisher.

1997 Barnes & Noble Books

ISBN 0-7607-0446-5

Printed and bound in the United States of America

99 00 01 M 9 8 7 6 5

QF

THE GLOVE OF DARTH VADER

PAUL DAVIDS
AND HOLLACE DAVIDS

Pencils by Benton Jew,
Industrial Light & Magic
Finished Art by Karl Kesel

The Rebel Alliance

Luke Skywalker

Princess Leia

Han Solo

Chewbacca

See-Threepio (C-3PO)

Artoo-Detoo (R2-D2)

Mon Mothma

Admiral Ackbar

The Empire

Trioculus

Grand Moff Hissa

Emdee-Five (MD-5)

Grand Moff Muzzer

Grand Moff Dunhausen

Grand Moff Thistleborn

Captain Dunwell

Aqualish Alien

To Jordan and Scott,
May the Force be with you . . .

A long time ago,
in a galaxy
far, far away...

The Adventure Continues . . .

It was an era of darkness, a time when the evil Empire ruled the galaxy. Fear and terror spread across every planet and moon.

Emperor Palpatine, the Imperial dictator, reigned, aided by his second-in-command, Darth Vader. Together they tried to crush all who resisted them—but still the Rebel Alliance survived.

The Rebel Alliance was formed by heroic men, women, and aliens, united against the Empire in their valiant fight to restore freedom and justice to the galaxy.

Luke Skywalker joined the Rebels after his uncle purchased a pair of droids known as See-Threepio (C-3PO) and Artoo-Detoo (R2-D2). The droids were on a mission to save the beautiful Princess Leia. Leia was a Rebel Alliance leader who was being held captive by the Empire, and was caught in the clutches of the evil Darth Vader.

In his quest to save Princess Leia, Luke was assisted by Han Solo, the dashing pilot of the spaceship *Millennium Falcon,* and Han's copilot, Chewbacca, a hairy alien known as a Wookiee.

Han and Luke eventually succeeded in rescuing the Rebel princess, but their struggle against the Empire did not end there. Luke and his ragtag group of Rebel freedom fighters battled armor-clad stormtroopers, and mile-long star destroyers, and faced the Empire's mightiest weapon of all—the Imperial Death Star. The Death Star was a battle station as big as a moon, with the power to destroy an entire planet. It was exploded by the Rebels in a deadly mission. The Empire soon built a second Death Star though, this one even larger and more powerful than the first.

In the course of his adventures Luke sought out the wise old hermit, Obi-Wan Kenobi, who became Luke's first teacher in the ways of the Jedi Knights.

The Jedi Knights, an ancient society of brave and noble warriors, were the protectors of the Old Republic in days before the Empire was formed. The Jedi believed that victory comes not just from physical strength but from a mysterious power called the Force.

The Force lies hidden deep within all things. It has two sides: one side that can be used for good, the other side a power of absolute evil.

In training to become a Jedi Knight, Obi-Wan Kenobi sent Luke to study under a great Jedi Master, Yoda. From Yoda, Luke discovered some startling truths about himself—Princess Leia was actually his twin sister and his father was none other than Darth Vader. Luke learned that Darth Vader had once been a Jedi Knight, but Vader was lured to the ways of the Dark Side by Emperor Palpatine and then became obsessed with power and consumed with hatred.

The Jedi Masters realized that it was Luke's destiny to battle his own father, or else the Dark Side would triumph. There were two confrontations between father and son, both of them duels fought with blazing lightsabers.

Before Darth Vader's death, Luke helped his father come to the understanding that Emperor Palpatine had turned him against everyone and everything he had ever loved. Darth Vader then destroyed the Emperor, hurling him down into the power core of the Death Star. Then the Death Star itself was destroyed, exploded in a Rebel attack.

With the Empire's evil leaders gone and their battle station destroyed, a new era has begun. Imperial warlords have been fighting for power among themselves, but no one knows who will seize control. However, the Prophets of the Dark Side have foretold that a new Emperor will soon arise, and on his hand he shall wear an indestructible symbol of evil—the glove of Darth Vader!

CHAPTER 1
Droids on a Mission

See-Threepio's frantic voice echoed through the Droid Repair Shop on Yavin Four, the fourth moon of the planet Yavin.

"But, Master Luke," Threepio was saying, "Kessel has always been *last* on my list of places in the galaxy I'd like to see. Particularly on a dangerous spy mission without my own head."

"You're only getting a different head *cover*, not a whole new head," Luke Skywalker said to his golden, human-shaped droid. He bent to examine a used droid head on a shelf. "We're not going to touch a single one of your microcircuits. We just don't want you to be noticed in a crowd of Kessel droids."

The Kessel droid head Luke was holding had a punched-in, evil-looking face. It was a face that didn't match Threepio's gentle personality at all. "What do you think of this one?" asked Luke.

"*That* one? There's something lacking in your taste, Master Luke. It's unsightly—and . . . and it's green!" Threepio stammered.

"Didn't I tell you about your new color-plating?"

"You're not going to make me green, are you?"

Threepio exclaimed, waving his arms.

"Don't panic," said Luke. "Your gold color will be restored, along with your usual head cover, when the mission is over. Come on, let's get started."

BZZZZZZZT!

Luke pressed his inter-office communications device, signaling the Droid Modification Team that Threepio was ready. The team was a group of Too-Onebee technical droids that specialized in repairing other droids and replacing their worn-out parts. The Too-Onebees brought with them Artoo-Detoo, a barrel-shaped droid that they had just finished modifying. Artoo now resembled a dark green Kessel mining droid, complete with a Kessel insignia on his dome.

"Dweeeet bchooo tzniiiiiiit!" beeped Artoo-Detoo, turning his new dome left and right so that Luke and Threepio would notice.

"No, I don't think you look wonderful," replied Threepio, who was an expert at translating six million galactic languages and understood all of Artoo's beeps, buzzes, and whistles.

Walking away from his little friend, Threepio reluctantly left with the Droid Modification Team. He returned an hour later.

"I hope you're satisfied," Threepio said with dismay.

"You look perfect," Luke replied with a smile. "Come on, we have to get to the new Senate. You don't want to miss the beginning of Mon Mothma's briefing, do you?"

Luke walked toward the door quickly, thinking to himself how fortunate the Alliance was to have a distinguished and brilliant woman like Mon Mothma as its leader. "When Mon Mothma explained our strategy for the battle against the Death Star, you were on time to hear her then—and this is no time to be late, either, Threepio. Especially since all of the key members of SPIN will be there."

SPIN was short for the Senate's Planetary Intelligence Network, a secret organization within the Alliance's new galactic government.

WHOOOOSH!

Luke's airspeeder zoomed over the treetops of the rain forest on Yavin Four, dodging the peaks of the old pyramids. Soon he could see many of the elaborate structures that had been built by a long-vanished race. He saw the Great Temple. And to his left the Temple of the Blueleaf Cluster. And up ahead the Palace of the Woolamander, where the new Senate met.

It was nearly twilight when Luke landed the airspeeder. He hurried Threepio and Artoo up the ramp to the main Senate entrance and they proceeded down a stone hallway until they reached the briefing room.

Seated at the conference table were two human women, two human men, and two aliens. The women were Mon Mothma and Princess Leia; the men were

Han Solo and Lando Calrissian, the governor of Cloud City on the planet Bespin; and the aliens were Chewbacca, the Wookiee, and Admiral Ackbar, the sad-eyed fishman and war hero from the watery world of Calamari.

Luke took his place at the center of the table, with Threepio and Artoo standing nearby.

"Well, kid," Han said to Luke, "you sure did a great job on these droids. If I didn't know what was going on, I'd swear I was on Kessel."

"Thanks, Han. Coming from you, that really means a lot," Luke said to his friend.

"Kessel is a planet that all experienced cargo pilots try to avoid," said Han. "Especially me. But a few times, when there was a fortune to be made from transporting spice, I flew the trip from Kessel anyway, against my better judgment. In fact, I've made the Kessel Run in the *Millennium Falcon* in less than twelve standard timeparts."

"You told me that the day I first met you, back in the cantina at the Mos Eisley spaceport on Tatooine," said Luke. "Remember? When I showed up with Obi-Wan Kenobi and—"

"Yeah, I remember, kid, now that you mention it," interrupted Han. He knitted his brows and frowned. "Well, take my word for it—things have gotten even meaner on Kessel since then. And it's tough times there for spice traders and old Corellian space pirates like me. These days, if they even *suspect* you might be loyal to the Alliance, they send you straight to the spice mines—to be a slave for life!"

"Which brings us to the urgency of the Kessel mission," Mon Mothma said strongly. "Thousands of grand moffs, evil warlords, stormtroopers, Imperial droids, and enemy officers from the Empire are arriving at Kessendra Stadium on Kessel for a big gathering in their capital city."

She turned to Artoo-Detoo and continued. "Artoo, your data banks now contain information on every important Imperial who might be at that meeting, including all those who may have ambitions to become the new leader of the Empire. You also have data on the Prophets of the Dark Side. There seems to be much controversy about the latest prophecy of the Supreme Prophet of the Dark Side, Kadann."

Mon Mothma touched a button on the conference table console and a holo-projector flashed Kadann's words in midair:

After Palpatine's fiery death
Another leader soon comes to command the Empire
And on his right hand he does wear
The glove of Darth Vader!

A menacing silence fell over the briefing room.

"*Ptooog bziiiini?*" beeped Artoo, as his new dome rotated back and forth.

"He wants to know how the right-hand glove of Darth Vader can still exist," said Threepio.

"Unlike the left-hand glove, the right glove was

made to be indestructible," Mon Mothma replied. "A symbol of evil that would survive forever. After Luke cut off Darth Vader's right hand in their lightsaber duel, the glove was believed to have been hurled out into space when the Death Star exploded.

"According to our intelligence reports," she continued, "the glove has not yet been found. We have teams out searching for it, but it's possible that someone at the Kessel meeting might have found the glove already and claim to be the new Emperor."

Suddenly Mon Mothma's holo-projector created an image of a meteor. "Threepio and Artoo, this may look like a meteor, but it's actually your landing pod," she explained. "Admiral Ackbar and his fellow Calamarians built this especially for your mission."

"We guarantee that it will do the job," Admiral

Ackbar said confidently.

Lando smiled and nudged his friend Han Solo, who was sitting beside him. "Han has been kind enough to offer me a ride back to Bespin," said Lando, "so that I can get back to Cloud City for some urgent business. On our way, as we pass near Kessel, we'll eject the pod from the *Millennium Falcon*, right, Han?"

"Sure thing," Han put in.

"The pod should get through enemy defenses undetected," said Mon Mothma, turning to the droids. "It's also been designed for your escape from Kessel. When your mission is over and you reboard, the pod will shed its meteor coating so that it will look like a spherical Imperial probe droid. Then it will automatically soar to the upper atmosphere, where you'll be picked up by an Imperial command speeder we captured and modified with hyperdrive for interplanetary flight—Command Speeder 714-D."

Threepio rubbed the back of his new metal head cover. He thought he could hear a fuse popping somewhere inside his electronic brain. This was all so shocking! "And what if we get lost on Kessel?" he asked timidly.

"You droids managed to find Jabba the Hutt's palace on Tatooine all by yourselves," Luke reminded Threepio.

"And you even helped rescue Han when he was frozen in suspended animation inside a block of solid carbonite," said Leia.

"*Grrrowff!*" Chewbacca agreed.

"On the outside chance that you droids do get lost," Mon Mothma added, "remember that we've programmed Artoo-Detoo's data banks with maps of Kessel that we recovered from an escaped slave. Those maps show every street in the capital city of Kessendra and the layout of Kessendra Stadium—even the slaves' secret escape tunnel you'll be using to get into the stadium."

At last Mon Mothma concluded the briefing and sent everyone to get a good night's rest before the mission began.

"Master Luke, sir," said Threepio in a sinking voice. "Are you sure there's no one else in the Alliance better suited for this mission than Artoo-Detoo and me?"

"You computed the odds yourself, Threepio," replied Luke. "I asked you what the chances are of any human or alien who's loyal to the Alliance getting back from Kessel alive."

Threepio nodded. "Only one chance in twelve thousand six hundred," he said, sighing. "Very well, then. It's all for the best. We droids are replaceable, after all."

Under the starlit sky of Yavin Four, Han Solo walked Princess Leia to her quarters.

"Your highness," said Han. "After Chewie and I drop off the droids in the meteor pod on Kessel and take Lando back to Cloud City . . . well, I don't know exactly how to put this . . . I'm not planning on coming back for a while."

"But, Han," Princess Leia protested, "you know how important you are to SPIN."

"Maybe so, but Lando's offered me a lease on a piece of sky near Cloud City. I've always dreamed of having a place of my own, and I figure it's about time Chewie and I built my dream sky house."

"Can't you put it off until we know what's going on with the new Emperor?" asked Leia.

"Princess, there's always something important that seems to come up before I can take care of my own dreams. Time is running out. And a man's got to do what he's got to do."

"If that's the way you want it, Han," Leia said, not quite understanding him. She turned away.

"I'm going to miss you, Princess," said Han, taking her hand. "May the Force be with you."

CHAPTER 2
Lightning Power of the Dark Side

As the *Millennium Falcon* came out of hyperdrive and slowed below lightspeed, Han and Chewie deliberately navigated into the heart of a huge electrical storm in Kessel's outer atmosphere. The black lightning clouds were an unsuspecting place from which to eject the meteor pod.

ZHWEEEEEK! The cargo door screeched as it opened.

Soon the pod was dropping toward Kessel, buffeted by strong winds, its outer rock-coating struck by lightning, its interior heated by friction. But it kept adjusting its path of descent, taking the droids to where they needed to go.

The worst part for Threepio and Artoo was the landing. The meteor pod bounced into a rocky mountainside, rolled into a few bushy Kesselian trees, and finally came to a stop within an easy walk to the hidden entrance of the slaves' escape tunnel.

The pod's hatch door opened and the two disguised droids emerged to face the looming moun-

tains set against an eerie pink sky. The electrical
storm had ended.

"I'm certainly glad droids don't get dizzy, or I
wouldn't be able to stand up for days," said Threepio.
He glanced at their pod. "Look, Artoo, our meteor
pod looks like just another boulder against the craggy
terrain. It should be safe here until we return. That is,
if we return."

They found the underground passageway, and
Threepio pushed away the rocks that concealed the
entrance. Soon they were heading into the tunnel,
which had a faint luminous glow from the many
spice-covered rocks.

In the semidarkness Threepio asked Artoo to
project Mon Mothma's holographic map of the tunnel interior. "That's upside down!" Threepio exclaimed. "Honestly, you don't expect me to stand on

my head to read that map, do you?"

Artoo flipped his projection so that the map was right-side up. After studying it, Threepio plunged ahead. With every clattering step, he took Artoo closer and closer to Kessendra Stadium, which was at the very edge of the capital city of this Imperial slave planet.

"Hurry—this way, Artoo!" said Threepio. "Mon Mothma's map said the entrance to the stadium is somewhere down here!"

"*Dweep booooooweep,*" beeped Artoo, rolling along as fast as he could.

"No, it isn't my fault that we're here," replied Threepio as he walked even faster. "We do have our orders, you know. Let's just hope that nobody finds out who we really are. Otherwise, they'll take us apart and use us for spare parts—or worse!"

Threepio continued talking without pause, since droids never have to stop to catch their breath the way organic creatures do. "It's positively horrifying. Half the Imperial officers in the galaxy are gathered together, practically right above our heads, and goodness knows what evil plans they're making."

Kessendra Stadium was the frequent site of gladiator games in which slaves fought to the death, while sportsmen from throughout the galaxy placed bets. Today, however, there would be no gladiator games.

"*Droot boopa zinnn,*" beeped Artoo.

"I quite agree with you," replied Threepio, nodding his head. "I'd have thought they'd given up the war, too, when their second Death Star blew up, and when Emperor Palpatine and Darth Vader died, and—Oh no!"

Threepio walked into a metal column and clattered to the ground. "Now look what you made me do." He quickly picked himself up and checked his plating for dents. "You're always distracting me, Artoo!"

Artoo gave a singsong series of toots and whistles. *"Reewooo dweet? Beeeeza zooon?"*

"No, there aren't any droid-eating monsters down here. Now stop babbling and help me look for the entrance to the stadium and— Gracious! There it is back there! Why didn't you tell me we'd

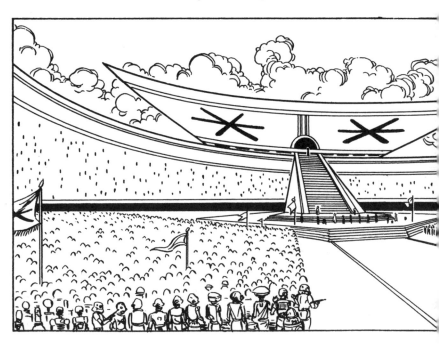

passed it, you nearsighted hunk of tin!"

"*Vrrrr BEEEEEP!*"

"Well, the same to you!"

Threepio cautiously opened the creaking metal door and sneaked out of the darkness, with Artoo rolling along behind him. The pink sky was so bright it nearly blinded Threepio's eye-sensors.

When his sensors cleared, Threepio could see that they were at the lower level of the stadium, where slaves and droids were gathered to listen to the speeches. All around them were green humanoid droids with menacing heads and barrel-shaped spice-mining droids, who looked just like Threepio and Artoo did in their disguises.

Above them, in the comfortable bleacher seats that surrounded the pit of slaves, were so many Imperial officers and stormtroopers that at first they all seemed to blur together. Artoo raised a long-distance sensor to get a close-up view. Then the barrel-shaped droid began matching the faces he saw with the faces and names of the Imperial officers in his data banks.

The crowd became quiet as a grand moff, one of the Empire's regional governors, began to speak. The beady-eyed grand moff was bald and his teeth had been filed into sharp, spearlike points.

"I am Grand Moff Hissa," he announced, just as Artoo figured out who he was. "And to my fellow grand moffs, and to the grand admirals, other officers, stormtroopers, bounty hunters, slavelords, and slaves, I bid you all Dark Greetings!

"We have gathered here today to mark a new beginning," he continued, puffing out his chest proudly to display his brown uniform. "The destruction of our latest Death Star was but a temporary setback. The Rebels have yet to see the full fury of our power and our might. We are developing even more advanced weapons, and when we are done, we shall rule the entire galaxy and *crush* the Rebel Alliance."

As he listened, Threepio whispered to Artoo. "Oh, dear, I certainly don't like the sound of this. No, I don't like the sound of this at all."

"The Central Committee of Grand Moffs has summoned you all here for this meeting to announce

our new leader," said Grand Moff Hissa in a bellow-
ing voice. "Even though Emperor Palpatine is dead,
his line continues. For many years you have heard
rumors that the Emperor had a son. But our departed
Emperor and the Central Committee of Grand Moffs
always denied those rumors, for reasons of Imperial
security. However, today I am authorized to inform
you that the Emperor *did* indeed have a son—a son
who shall be our new chosen one!"

The stadium was filled with gasps of shock and
surprise at this revelation.

"The Emperor's son has lived among you on
Kessel for many years now, keeping his true identity
a carefully guarded secret," Grand Moff Hissa con-
tinued. "And now at last the time has come for the
Emperor's son to take his rightful place as heir to the
Empire."

"Who is the Emperor's son?" shouted a grand
admiral.

There was a suspenseful moment of silence.

Then a huge, black door suddenly opened, and
a tall mutant dressed in black came out to face the
gathering.

"Friends of the Empire," Grand Moff Hissa an-
nounced, "I present to you the son of Emperor
Palpatine—Trioculus, the Supreme Slavelord of
Kessel!"

But instead of cheering, a frightened hush crept
through the crowd at the sight of the new ruler.
Trioculus was known to be a ruthless and merciless

slavelord, one who had sent many slaves to their deaths.

Threepio could see that Trioculus looked powerful and threatening. But he was surprised that he wasn't ugly like Darth Vader and Emperor Palpatine had been. In fact, Trioculus was almost handsome. Except for one thing—

Two of Trioculus's eyes were right where Threepio expected them to be, on either side of his nose. However, it was Trioculus's third eye, right in the middle of his forehead, that made him look rather unusual.

Threepio bent down to talk quietly to Artoo. "A mutant—part human, part alien," he said. "Quite surprising. I've certainly never heard any gossip that Emperor Palpatine had a son by a three-eyed alien woman. Have you?"

From Artoo's beeps and buzzes, Threepio quickly learned many things he had never known before. For instance, Artoo's data banks revealed that some old Imperial stormtroopers *did* believe that the Emperor had had a son with three eyes, a son who lived on Kessel. However, when the Rebel Alliance had investigated that story, no evidence had ever been found. Now, however, the Alliance would have to investigate the situation again.

Artoo's rapid beeps revealed more about Trioculus, information from Mon Mothma's secret Alliance files on the slavelords of the Kessel spice mines.

Trioculus had a reputation for being among the

most evil and cruel of the Kessel slavelords, personality traits that developed when Trioculus was just a child. As the only mutant in his school on Kessel, he was teased and hit constantly by the other students who made fun of his third eye. Trioculus became obsessed with fighting back and taking revenge. He became the schoolyard bully, and he learned how to make his classmates fear him, by spying on them and reporting those who didn't follow the rules.

As Trioculus grew older, he studied the history of warfare and Imperial military tactics. That was when he had first become devoted to gaining total control over both his enemies and his friends.

Trioculus had few friends. But it was the quality of his allies that counted, not the quantity. Through his study of warfare he had won friends among important Imperial officers—especially the spike-toothed Grand Moff Hissa, who respected Trioculus's total loyalty to the Imperial cause.

And so, as one of Grand Moff Hissa's pets, Trioculus had come up from the ranks of overseers of the spice mines. Soon afterward, again with Grand Moff Hissa's help, Trioculus had been appointed Lord Overseer and Supreme Slavelord.

The crowd continued to watch in hushed silence, as Trioculus began to speak in a cold, throaty voice. "My father, the Emperor, had many powers of the Dark Side. But without three eyes he could never achieve perfection. It was known by the ancients that a Dark Lord with three eyes has a secret strength possessed by none other. And so it is my destiny to rule over my father's Empire and bring us the glory that he never achieved!"

Grand Moff Hissa came forward. "We have heard from Trioculus, the Emperor's son, and we shall obey him, one and all! Prepare to bow and accept your new Emperor!"

A member of the Imperial Royal Guard stood up and shouted out a troublesome question in a booming voice.

"Just a moment, Grand Moff Hissa!" said the bold and foolhardy Royal Guard member. "Lord Trioculus, are you aware that there are others who claim to be the new ruler of the Empire? I have been to the planet Gargon. There, Grand Admiral Grunger says *he* is our new leader. And *he* has a fleet of thirty star destroyers!"

"I shall deal with him when I am ready," Trioculus said. "He will learn who is the rightful Emperor!"

Then an admiral stood to speak. "How can you claim to be the new chosen one when you do not wear Darth Vader's glove? The Prophets of the Dark Side have said that the next Emperor shall wear—"

"As the Emperor's son," shouted Trioculus, "it is through my blood that I rule, not with some glove!"

"But the Prophets of the Dark Side are powerful!" declared the member of the Imperial Royal Guard. "They foretold that the Rebels would blow up both Death Stars—and they even knew *when* they would be destroyed. They saw the future. Therefore they must know our destiny!"

"Only *I* know the destiny of the Empire," thundered Trioculus, "and only *I* have the power of my father and more—including the lightning power of the Dark Side!"

Trioculus raised his arms and bolts of lightning shot from his fingertips. The lightning crackled in two directions, striking both the member of the Imperial Royal Guard and the grand admiral who dared to question him.

The men fell to their knees, pleading with Trioculus to stop as they quaked and thrashed on the ground, moaning, while the electricity sizzled all around them.

At last Trioculus showed mercy on them and lowered his hands. "Now who will be the first officer to step forward and pledge his loyalty to me?" he demanded.

"I will!" shouted a general.

"No, let it be me!" shouted a grand moff. He rushed forward to be the first to bow down before Trioculus, and Trioculus accepted him.

After Trioculus listened to the officers pledge their vows of loyalty, he raised his arms, turned his back, and left through the huge black door. Grand Moff Hissa followed him.

Throughout the stadium everyone was talking about what they had just seen.

"I think we'd better get out of here, Artoo."

Threepio turned to look for the little droid. "Hey, wait for me!" he said, noticing that Artoo was already heading back toward the entrance to the underground passageway.

Threepio hurried to catch up with Artoo. As they approached the door to the tunnel, they saw that it was surrounded by stormtroopers—and the stormtroopers were bolting it shut!

CHAPTER 3
The Seven Words of Trioculus

Trioculus, surrounded by stormtrooper bodyguards, departed from Kessendra Stadium with Grand Moff Hissa. He was also accompanied by Emdee-Five (MD-5), his droid with a narrow head and shining eyes.

They rode in an armored landspeeder limousine to the large, black metal palace where Trioculus had lived since his promotion to Lord Overseer and Supreme Slavelord of the Spice Mines.

Upon their arrival Emdee went directly to the huge kitchen to warn Trioculus's chef to complete the preparations for the celebration banquet.

Soon Trioculus and Grand Moff Hissa were joined by a small, select group of grand moffs loyal to Trioculus and a grand admiral from the planet Gargon. Together they sat at a very long banquet table while a servant brought in trays filled with Whaladon meat, a delicacy that was reserved only for the Imperial ruling class and forbidden to stormtroopers and slaves. Whaladon meat was especially prized because it was thought to be a source of strength.

Whaladons were huge whale-like creatures, mammals that lived only in the oceans of the watery planet Calamari. They were highly intelligent and wise, and it was against the laws of Calamari to kill them. Still, a huge, illegal Whaladon hunting operation existed in Calamari's waters. In fact, even though Whaladons were an endangered species, there were more Whaladon hunters on Calamari than ever before, led by Captain Dunwell, a trusted friend of the Central Committee of Grand Moffs.

After Trioculus and his guests finished their dinner and while dessert was being served, Grand Moff Hissa announced that the new Emperor had something important to tell them. The guests became silent as Trioculus, who was in the place of honor at the head of the table, stood and drew himself up to his full, towering height.

He spoke seven words.

"Find me the glove of Darth Vader!" he said in a

booming voice. Then he stared at them with his third eye, causing his loyal officers to shudder.

Grand Moff Hissa understood the difficult task before them. The Central Committee of Grand Moffs had declared Trioculus to be the new Emperor. But if someone else found the glove and wore it, then Kadann, the Supreme Prophet of the Dark Side, might declare that Trioculus was not the rightful heir to the throne and should be deposed.

If that happened, the Central Committee of Grand Moffs would lose their credibility and would probably also lose their influence and power in running the Empire. Grand Moff Hissa was determined, at any cost, not to let that happen. In fact, all friends and allies of the Central Committee of Grand Moffs were being notified immediately that if any of them found the glove, he or she should notify Trioculus and turn it over to him at once.

To the other grand moffs, Hissa said: "We have heard our leader's words, and we shall do as he says. From each of your planets you will send out probe droids to search for the glove of Darth Vader. I shall send probes to search the forest moon of Endor and the space that surrounds it, scanning the area where the Death Star exploded."

Grand Moff Muzzer, who was the plumpest and most round-faced of the grand moffs, spoke his mind. "Space is vast and the glove very small. Perhaps you expect too much of the Empire's probe droids."

"Probe droids can find a bomb that's no bigger

than a man's hand," replied Grand Moff Hissa, "so they should have no trouble finding a glove. Especially one that is indestructible."

"We will need a new, secret home base," said Trioculus, turning his attention to another matter of business. "I have yet to decide where. I will now hear your suggestions."

Several of the grand moffs squirmed in their seats. This was new to them, entirely new. Emperor Palpatine had never asked them for suggestions.

A few moments passed before one of the grand moffs grew bold enough to speak. "I suggest the planet Tatooine," said Grand Moff Dunhausen, who wore earrings, little ornaments shaped like laser pistols. "We can take over the Mos Eisley spaceport!"

Trioculus dismissed the idea immediately. "That useless planet where Jabba the Hutt died? Do you think I want the Empire to waste its time eliminating sand people like the Tusken Raiders and those two-bit traders, the jawas?"

There was a longer silence before the next suggestion came. "Bespin!" said Grand Moff Thistleborn, whose bushy eyebrows touched each other in the middle and curled up at the ends. "Let's take over Cloud City!"

Trioculus sneered. "We already have a barge full of factories for building weapons and mining tibanna gas on Bespin. Besides, Cloud City isn't a fit place to train our troops."

"Dagobah?" offered the grand admiral from Gargon.

"You're wasting my time!" Trioculus shouted, slamming his fist down on the table. The dishes rattled and a serving flask of zoochberry cream fell on its side.

"Hoth?" Grand Moff Hissa said hesitantly.

Trioculus's scowl changed to a sly smile. "Very good, Grand Moff Hissa," he said. "You suggest the coldest, most miserable of all the frozen ice planets. Give me your reasoning."

"The new base should be located on a world that the Rebel Alliance wouldn't consider important," Grand Moff Hissa began. "Preferably a world where Imperial stormtroopers won't be too comfortable— comfortable men grow lazy and rebellious. There are still bases and military bunkers on Hoth that the Rebels once used before our four-legged AT-AT walkers chased them off the planet," he continued. "All we have to do is move in!"

Trioculus gave the order.

All loyal warlords would transport their Imperial military equipment to Hoth—the strike cruisers, frigates, and shuttles; the star galleons and star destroyers; the torpedo spheres and mobile command bases; the four-legged AT-AT snow-walkers, probe droids, and hoverscouts. Everything!

The grand admiral from Gargon suddenly rose to his feet. "You can't do this, Trioculus!" he shouted. "You're being too hasty. Until you find the glove of

Darth Vader, you won't be accepted as the new Emperor. What if Grand Admiral Grunger finds it first and—"

ZING!

The grand admiral fell forward onto the banquet table and spoke no more.

The grand moffs looked from one to the other with raised eyebrows. Most of them had expected the lightning power from Trioculus's fingertips to kill the grand admiral. But it wasn't Trioculus's style to exert himself to execute just anyone. He had instructed Grand Moff Hissa to take care of that kind of dirty work, especially in the case of a traitor interfering with a high-level Imperial conference.

And so the deed was done by Hissa with one short blast from his sidearm laser pistol.

Threepio and Artoo were lost on the streets of Kessendra. Unable to exit the stadium the same way they had entered it, they quickly joined the flow of droids streaming away from the event, hoping they wouldn't be noticed. Walking around the city, they hadn't found one street sign that matched the information in Artoo's data banks.

"*Tzoooooot gniiiiizba!*" Artoo beeped in frustration.

"Calm down, Artoo, there must be some mistake," said Threepio. "We'll find our way."

"*Chpeeeeeeez phooooooch!*" tooted Artoo.

"Then let's go down to the next street and check that one," replied Threepio, heading south.

"*Pchoook ftiiiiz mebiiiiing kniiiiish!*" Artoo beeped noisily when they came to the next sign.

Threepio shook his head in dismay. "Slavelord Boulevard. No, this definitely isn't Spice Mines Avenue. It seems that all these streets have been renamed since Mon Mothma got that data."

The two droids wandered along the twisting streets of the city. The boulevards were bustling with stormtroopers and spice transport vehicles went bouncing past. As Threepio and Artoo crossed an avenue, they were almost run over by some Imperial officers who were riding in a landspeeder limousine.

After hours of going around in circles, Threepio and Artoo finally made their way out of the capital city to the very edge of the mountains that were filled with spice mines.

"I wasn't cut out to be a spy," Threepio declared as he finally located a path through the Kesselian trees. "I should go back to working with binary load lifters. That was my first job. I'm still not sure why I left."

"*Deeeeewooop broooop!*" tooted Artoo. A tiny radar screen popped out of the little droid's head and began swiftly spinning around.

"I certainly *hope* we get back to Yavin Four," replied Threepio. "Master Luke is going to blow a short circuit when he hears the news about the Emperor's son!"

"Tzoooooch briiiiiiiib!"

"Now what are you beeping about, you hysterical bag of bolts?"

SHIBOOOOOM!

Threepio looked up at the pink sky to see an Imperial command speeder that looked just like the one that was supposed to pick them up. But Artoo confirmed its number was not 714-D, so there was no reason to assume it was friendly.

And soon there wasn't just one command speeder, there were three—then four of them!

They seemed to be flying close to the mountains, looking for something.

Threepio began calculating the odds that they were searching for a certain meteor pod and two particular droids. He shook his head in dismay when he realized the chances were 1,245 to 1 that the Imperials had figured out they were there.

Threepio led Artoo behind a giant boulder, where they could peek out at the craggy, rocky meteor pod that had brought them to Kessel. But no sooner had the droids begun looking at their pod than a command speeder began shooting laserblasts at the surrounding boulders.

"I have a very bad feeling about this, Artoo," Threepio said grimly.

A blast suddenly struck the pod, exploding it into scrap metal right in front of the droids' eye-sensors.

"Oh, nooooooo!" said Threepio frantically.

Within moments, Threepio's bad feeling got

worse, as he watched an Imperial command speeder land near the exploded pod. Stormtroopers got out and began to inspect the debris.

"We're doomed," said Threepio.

"Get down, you two!" said a familiar-sounding voice.

Threepio turned and nearly stumbled in shock as a man in a green slave robe pulled back his hood and revealed his face.

"Master Luke! You found us. Oh, thank goodness! But what are you doing here?"

"Looking for you two. When there was no sign of your pod taking off, Admiral Ackbar and I figured you droids might be in need of some help. We took a big gamble by landing. Quick—this way!"

The droids followed Luke Skywalker into the Kesselian mountain forest. Moments later they ar-

rived at the Imperial command speeder that the Alliance had captured—Command Speeder 714-D—which was waiting for them.

Once they were safely inside, they greeted Admiral Ackbar, who was at the controls, and quickly blasted off.

The other Imperial command speeders followed them, firing at them from behind.

Ackbar and Luke returned the fire. They made a series of spectacular direct hits. One after another their enemies made crash dives, spinning out of control, back to the surface of Kessel.

As their spaceship soared away from the outer atmosphere of Kessel, Artoo's radar screen popped up and spun around quickly. *"Bzzz tzzzt gniiiz bzheeep dzz dzooop!"* he beeped urgently.

"Oh, dear," said Threepio. "Artoo definitely doesn't advise that we chart a direct course back to Yavin Four. He's spotted Imperial probe droids directly in our path!"

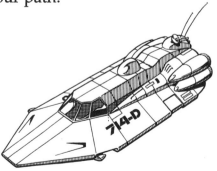

CHAPTER 4
Endangered Whaladons

Hundreds of probe droids with clawlike arms searched through space for the glove of Darth Vader.

While he waited for the reports from these probe droids, Trioculus delayed moving the Imperial forces to the bleak ice world of Hoth.

Soon news began trickling in.

The probe droids found everything but what Trioculus wanted most. They found debris from the Death Star, runaway prisoners, unexploded bombs, Alliance starships, and bounty hunters who were stealing Imperial weapons. They even spotted the missing Imperial Command Speeder 714-D, which narrowly got away when it changed course and entered a dangerous, radioactive asteroid zone from which few spaceships had ever escaped.

But there was still no sign of the glove of Darth Vader.

Trioculus released his fury by hunting giant fefze beetles in the Kesselian mountains. He managed to kill three giant fefze, and with each conquest Grand Moff Hissa congratulated him enthusiastically.

But still Trioculus wasn't satisfied. In an angry

voice he spoke of wanting a bigger hunt, a bigger kill. He proposed a journey to the steaming, ammonia-filled jungles of the planet Cona to hunt star dragons. However, before Grand Moff Hissa could even ask about arranging such a safari, Trioculus quickly changed the subject.

"Have any more troops questioned my right to be the new Emperor?" he asked.

"Some of the stormtroopers have been heard to complain, Lord Trioculus," replied Grand Moff Hissa.

"I want their names," Trioculus boomed, exploding with anger. "Their treason shall be punished!"

"Yes, your lordship." Grand Moff Hissa searched his mind for something new to report. "I also thought you should know that a salvage spaceship found what was thought to be a glove this morning. Unfortunately it turned out to be nothing but an old, rusted droid hand, floating in space in a cloud of hydrogen gas."

"Don't speak to me of droid hands, Hissa," said Trioculus, sneering. "My patience for this search is nearing an end."

Shortly after they returned to Trioculus's sleek black palace, a shipment of Whaladon meat was delivered to the palace kitchen. The delivery agent had come directly from the Kessel spaceport, where the meat had arrived in an Imperial carrack cruiser filled with cargo from the planet Calamari.

The agent bowed before Grand Moff Hissa, who accepted the delivery papers.

"I've also brought a message for Lord Trioculus from Captain Dunwell," said the delivery agent. He broke the seal on the small case he was carrying, took out a hologram disk, and handed it to Grand Moff Hissa, who in turn handed it over directly to Trioculus.

"See that no one disturbs me while I find out what Captain Dunwell has to say," ordered the three-eyed ruler.

Trioculus took the disk into one of his private chambers and inserted it into a holo-projector. Within moments the face of Captain Dunwell appeared as a holographic image, floating before him.

Captain Dunwell had a short white beard and a reddish, leathery face. He wore a blue naval uniform with shiny buttons and rows of medals.

"Dark Greetings, Lord Trioculus," he began. "Here, beneath the oceans of Calamari, I have made an astounding discovery. The Central Committee of Grand Moffs instructed me to contact you directly about this matter. As you may know, I have always been a loyal friend of the grand moffs. I urge you to come to see me on Calamari at once, at the Whaladon Processing Center. Your lordship will not be disappointed!"

Beneath the oceans of Calamari, Leviathor, the huge, white leader of the Whaladons, swam to the newly created Whaladon graveyard. In just a few years the bones of so many Whaladons had been dumped there by Captain Dunwell's Whaladon hunters that the sea floor in that region was now white.

Leviathor beheld the jagged rim of a crater just beyond the seaweed forest. Even from afar he could hear the dreaded machines churning in the huge underwater building at the bottom of that crater. The building was known as the Whaladon Processing Center.

Leviathor knew all too well that it was here where Captain Dunwell and his walrus-faced crew of Aqualish aliens killed the Whaladons that they captured.

There were now many young Whaladons who had no mothers to nurse them. And there were many older Whaladons, who used to swim the oceans of Calamari freely, who now hid, fearing for their

lives, in the darkness of undersea caves.

Swishing his great tail fin, Leviathor felt an invisible fire burning within him as he remembered the many learned and wise Whaladons who were now gone forever. No longer would they teach or sing songs—there was nothing left of them but their bones. Leviathor knew he had to save his endangered species before it was too late.

Just then a bright yellow light flashed behind Leviathor. He had been targeted. They were coming for *him* now!

The mighty Whaladon turned in the water and saw the huge new vessel—the biggest Whaladon-

hunting submarine ever built—tracking him, following him with his every dive.

Leviathor raced for his life, his huge heart pounding fast.

There was a roar behind him and the water swirled with foam. A great suction was pulling at his tail, suction as if from a whirlpool.

Leviathor dove again. Swimming as he had never swum before, he sailed into the seaweed forest and down into a wide coral cave.

There he hid until the death machine had passed by. Then Leviathor swam toward the Domed City of Aquarius, the undersea center of civilization on Calamari. He had to find someone who could help the Whaladons, and soon!

Aboard Command Speeder 714-D the recently installed shield that protected the spaceship against radioactivity did its job. It helped Luke and Admiral Ackbar navigate safely out of the dangerous asteroid zone, where they had maneuvered to get away from the prying eye-sensors of the Imperial probe droids.

"We'll go to Calamari, Luke," Admiral Ackbar said as he programmed the command speeder on an automatic course toward his home planet. "When we get there, we'll transfer Artoo-Detoo's spy data about Trioculus and the Imperial officers into a computer that will analyze it."

"But Mon Mothma and Princess Leia are waiting for that information *now"* said Luke.

"At the moment we're likely to be spotted by Imperials if we fly near Yavin Four," explained Ackbar. "We'll wait on Calamari for a while, then send a Calamarian cargo cruiser òn ahead of us with the coded data."

"When we get to Calamari," Threepio asked anxiously, "will there be time for Artoo and me to be modified back to our usual-looking selves at the Droid Repair Shop in the Domed City of Aquarius?"

"Are you sure that's what you want, Threepio?" said Luke with a grin. "I'm sort of getting used to you being green—and mean-looking."

"Honestly, Master Luke, sometimes your sense of humor astounds me."

A short time later when they came out of hyperdrive in the region of Calamari, Admiral Ackbar contacted Pisces Base, one of the Calamarian cities on a platform that floated on the ocean. He alerted Pisces that Imperial Command Speeder 714-D was a friendly ship of the Alliance and requested permission to land.

From Pisces Base Admiral Ackbar took Luke, Threepio, and Artoo aboard a Calamarian shuttle submarine that was heading for the Domed City of Aquarius.

Though there were many other cities on platforms above the waters, the Domed City of Aquarius was the only one that was located entirely under the sea. It was encased in a gigantic bubble, with the lower half containing rocks, coral, canals, and seawater and the upper half containing air. In Aquarius air-breathers and water-breathers lived above and below one another, in a spirit of brotherhood and equality.

The Calamarian shuttle sub approached the domed city and entered the wide undersea tunnel entrance. Then it surfaced inside the bubble and docked.

As the spy mission team disembarked, Admiral Ackbar stopped suddenly. Luke wondered what was wrong. Finally Ackbar said, "Listen to that sound— it's a Whaladon song."

Luke noticed it, too. It was a faint, haunting melody, echoing between the tall buildings on both sides of the biggest canal in the city.

Making his way through the crowd, Ackbar led Luke and the droids toward the canal. There they saw Leviathor, his big white humps sticking out of the water.

Admiral Ackbar was one of the few air-breathing fishmen who understood Whaladon songs. As Leviathor sang about how the Whaladons were threatened with extinction because of Captain Dunwell's new Whaladon-hunting submarine, the admiral hung his head in sorrow.

"Wise One of the Calamarian Seas," said Admiral Ackbar, "you have my solemn promise that I will do everything I can to save you and your valiant species."

"Tell him he has my promise, too," Luke Skywalker added.

CHAPTER 5
Captain Dunwell's Discovery

Intent on learning what Captain Dunwell had found, Trioculus left for Calamari in an Imperial strike cruiser that had been modified to travel both in outer space and undersea.

Soon after the strike cruiser penetrated the atmosphere of Calamari, it plunged underwater. In the cruiser's forward observation room Trioculus peered with all three of his eyes at the misty, dark ocean bottom.

He could make out the outline of a crater. And moments later, inside the crater on the ocean floor, he could see the faint white outline of Captain Dunwell's Whaladon Processing Center.

"We're in contact with Captain Dunwell, sir," said Grand Moff Hissa. "He's planning to greet you with a thirty laser-cannon salute and a military procession."

"Absolutely not," said Trioculus in a stern voice. "If I had wanted to be noticed, I would have asked for a parade, not a private meeting."

"As you wish, my Emperor."

As the Imperial strike cruiser approached the

Whaladon Processing Center, Trioculus could see Captain Dunwell's new, immense Whaladon-hunting submarine stationed at an open undersea docking bay.

"It's equipped with whirlpool generators," explained Grand Moff Hissa, "for sucking the Whaladons right out of the ocean and into big storage chambers. The generators are powered by an anti-matter furnace,"

"Impressive," said Trioculus.

As the Imperial strike cruiser entered another of the docking bays at the huge underwater facility, Grand Moff Hissa assisted Trioculus's crew with the docking procedures.

GRONGGGG!

A clang sounded as a large metal door closed behind Trioculus's Imperial strike cruiser. Then seawater was quickly pumped out of the docking bay, making it safe for Trioculus, Grand Moff Hissa, and the droid Emdee to climb out and enter the Whaladon Processing Center.

There they were met by Captain Dunwell, who knelt on one knee and bowed his head before the Imperial leader. "Lord Trioculus," he said, "a most Imperial welcome to you." Then he glanced up and smiled proudly.

Trioculus didn't like the way the captain seemed to be staring at him. It was as though the captain were repulsed by Trioculus's third eye.

"I trust you had a safe and comfortable journey," Captain Dunwell offered, nervously tweaking his short white beard.

"You need not worry about my comfort," replied Trioculus. "I want to know what was so urgent that I had to come all the way to Calamari for you to show it to me."

"Certainly, your lordship," said the captain, fidgeting with the medals on his bright blue uniform. "Come, we should speak in the privacy of my office."

Together they climbed up some stairs, then walked along a metal balcony that overlooked an enormous work area. Down below, dozens of Aqualish were skinning several Whaladons that had been killed, chopping the meat into huge slabs and loading it into carts.

The walrus-faced alien race of Aqualish, who had smooth, tough skins and large eyes, was a stubborn and tough fighting breed. They worked as bounty hunters, mercenaries, and as ruthless Whaladon killers.

The Whaladon meat they were chopping would soon be transported to the Whaladon Meat Quality Control Division.

Trioculus's three eyes peered down at the workers as he walked slowly from one end of the balcony to the other. He nodded approvingly, but his mind was on other things. In fact, he was in such an impatient mood that his right hand had begun twitching.

"I hope you're finding this instructive," said Captain Dunwell. "My office is just a little farther."

They continued walking through cold corridors and across wide work platforms until they reached the building's largest office, which belonged to Captain Dunwell. It had a gigantic window with a wide, sweeping view of the ocean and its enormous seaweed forest containing exotic Calamarian fish of every size, color, and shape imaginable.

When the Imperial leader entered the office, followed by Grand Moff Hissa and Emdee, Captain Dunwell locked the door and pointed to a navigation chart.

"This chart shows the route I took when I made my last journey to the Valley of the Giant Oysters, located on the other side of the Seascape Mountains. And this area here," Captain Dunwell continued, pointing out a small region of the undersea valley, "is where I discovered debris from an explosion."

The captain showed Trioculus the few metal scraps that were on his desk. "This is some of the debris I brought back with me. I've had it analyzed by an engineer—it's from the Death Star. I could hardly believe it since the Death Star blew up millions of miles away, near Endor."

"The intense gravity of black holes and other interstellar forces cause warps, folds, and buckles in space," explained Grand Moff Hissa. "Asteroids and spaceships have tumbled into these space warps and have suddenly reappeared millions of miles away. The same thing must have happened to this debris from the Imperial Death Star."

"Enough theories, Hissa," said Trioculus. "Continue with your story, Captain Dunwell."

He stared at the captain with his third eye, sending out hypnotic waves. A stare like that could make a man very truthful. The captain turned slightly pale.

"One of the chunks of the Death Star lying in the valley was huge—bigger than a Y-wing fighter, all melted and fused in a twisted shape. It was too large to bring back in the vessel I was in, so I suited up and examined it on the ocean floor. I tried to blast a hole in it, but my small laser couldn't do the job.

"I suspected that it was hollow, so I used my portable X-ray scanner to find out what was inside," he went on. "Allow me to show you what the scanner revealed."

The captain opened a drawer and took out several X-ray negatives. He studied first one image, then another, and then another. "Here," he said at last. "Look at this one." He touched his forefinger to the shadowy negative.

Trioculus leaned forward for a closer look.

Shutting his two lower eyes, he stared at the image with his third eye. The spot that Captain Dunwell was touching showed an object that seemed to have five fingers. Was it a hand? Or a glove?

Trioculus glanced at his right hand, which was trembling once again as he dreamed of fulfilling his goal. No human hand could have survived the heat of the Death Star explosion, he thought. And only one glove was known to be totally indestructible. This had to be it. A short undersea journey away. Almost within his grasp.

"You were correct to request that I come here, Captain," said Trioculus. "You have done well."

"Thank you, your lordship," said the captain, his voice booming with pride.

"How soon can you get us to the Valley of the Giant Oysters?" asked Grand Moff Hissa.

"I'll tell my crew to power up the Whaladon-hunting submarine immediately," Captain Dunwell replied.

Even sooner than Trioculus had expected, they were ready to depart.

KRR-RR—AAAAAAANG!

With a mighty roar the Whaladon-hunting submarine pushed away from its undersea dock. Bubbling foam churned behind it as the huge submarine picked up speed.

Captain Dunwell pointed out to Trioculus each of the vessel's special features.

Trioculus's face darkened with a nasty smile. "With so much advanced technology aboard, you'll have to make sure this ship is never captured by the Rebel Alliance."

"Have no fear of that, Lord Trioculus," replied Captain Dunwell. "If there's ever an undersea battle on Calamari, I'll destroy this ship myself before I'll ever let it fall into the hands of the Rebels."

* * *

Luke Skywalker's heart was pounding with excitement as Threepio translated Artoo's high-pitched beeps. All of Artoo's intelligence data about the meeting of Imperials in Kessendra Stadium was now at Luke's fingertips.

Luke and Admiral Ackbar soon hurried to the Calamarian office of SPIN. For months Luke had received intelligence reports about the Empire's many denials concerning the rumor that Emperor Palpatine had had a son. But at the big Imperial meeting in Kessendra Stadium the Empire had suddenly admitted that all its denials had been false. Just thinking about it made Luke shake his head in frustration. How could anyone believe *anything* the Empire said, when the Empire changed the "official truth" day by day to suit its convenience?

While Luke and Admiral Ackbar took care of the urgent business of contacting Mon Mothma about Trioculus, Threepio and Artoo checked into the Droid Repair Shop.

Threepio was given another head cover that was exactly like his old one, except that this one was shinier, without any scratches, nicks, or dents. He admired his replating job, looking at his golden color from every angle.

Artoo-Detoo also underwent a change back to his usual color. But it was his brand-new blue and silver R2 dome that made the little barrel-shaped droid spin in circles, showing how happy he was to be back to normal.

When the droids came out of the Droid Repair Shop, Luke, Threepio, and Artoo boarded a fish-shaped Calamarian minisub with Admiral Ackbar, who navigated the vessel toward the ocean floor.

"Now that we've sent the news to Mon Mothma about the Imperial leader Trioculus, it's time we tried to help the Whaladons," Ackbar told them. "And the best way for me to explain the Whaladon crisis is to show you the Whaladon graveyard. From there it's a short trip to Captain Dunwell's undersea Whaladon Processing Center."

"*Dzneeeeek?*" beeped Artoo.

"Artoo wants to know what they do there," translated Threepio.

"That's where they take the captured Whaladons and butcher them," said Admiral Ackbar. "There they turn those beautiful, intelligent creatures into food for Imperial officers!"

"Perish the thought," said Threepio, shaking his head in dismay.

"For many years we've had a law on Calamari making it illegal to hunt Whaladons," explained Admiral Ackbar. "But no matter how hard we try we cannot control Captain Dunwell. He does whatever the Central Committee of Grand Moffs wants, and they want Whaladon meat, even if it means destroying the ecology of Calamari."

"*Chnooozbch kjiiik?*" beeped Artoo.

"Artoo wants to know how the hunting of Whaladons harms the ecology of your planet,"

Threepio translated.

"The Whaladons eat the little plants, or plankton, that grow at the surface of our oceans," Ackbar explained. "If those little plants spread and become too plentiful, as they breathe they could use up all the carbon dioxide in our atmosphere—the process of photosynthesis. Without carbon dioxide our planet would get much colder. You see, we need Whaladons to keep the amount of plankton in balance, or we Calamarians could wake up one day to find ourselves in an ice age!"

Admiral Ackbar's attention was suddenly captured by a blip on his sonar unit. "Luke, have a look at this," he said in a serious tone. He pointed to a bright circle of luminous light on the sonar screen. "The only vessel of this size in these waters is Captain Dunwell's submarine. Let's see what he's up to."

Cautiously the Calamarian minisub followed the huge, dark shape lurking dead ahead. Light from luminous coral began reflecting off the Whaladon-hunting submarine, making its dark form more vis-

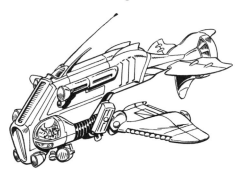

ible. Luke could see that the vessel was like a vast self-propelled underwater fortress.

The Calamarian minisub followed it silently, navigating the same course at a safe distance to the rear. The small size and efficient antisonar system of the Calamarian minisub made it almost impossible for an enemy to detect, except at very close range.

In the cramped cabin Luke Skywalker watched through the front porthole. Threepio was tightly strapped into the rear seat, beneath the emergency navigation controls, and Artoo was pushed up against the golden droid's knees.

Luke could see the white form of Leviathor leading a group of Whaladons away from the path of the dreaded submarine. Then he choked with horror as he saw a swirling mass of foaming dark water, like an undersea tornado, moving straight toward Leviathor.

Admiral Ackbar struggled to control his little sub as it vibrated wildly in the churning water. Luke watched as Leviathor tried to escape, but the whirlpool caught hold of Leviathor as the old white Whaladon fought for his life.

The suction pulled Leviathor backward, tail first. Then Leviathor spun around and around at a dizzying speed, while a huge door opened on the side of the Whaladon-hunting submarine. In a few moments Leviathor was sucked through the door and he vanished from sight.

THUUUU-WHOMP!

As the metal door slammed shut, claiming its

prize catch, Luke could hear a dull thud pounding through the waves.

"This is a very sad day for Calamari," said Ackbar, shuddering. "Without Leviathor the Whaladons haven't a chance now."

Luke's mouth fell open as he saw another Whaladon trapped in the whirlpool. The Whaladon fell into the swirling hole, tumbling and twisting, then was quickly trapped inside another storage chamber.

Then a third Whaladon was trapped.

And a fourth.

Ackbar abruptly pushed the steering lever to the left. Their Calamarian minisub turned sharply away, then picked up speed.

"Surely there must be something we can do," said Threepio, nervously polishing his fingers. "Why, they've swallowed up four Whaladons in the last few minutes, including Leviathor."

"It looks hopeless," said Ackbar sadly.

Luke remembered all of the hopeless situations he had been in before. How many times in his life had he almost been ready to give up? But he never had.

If there was any hope of saving the Whaladons, they couldn't turn back now. So they kept following the Whaladon-hunting submarine as it went straight toward the dark Seascape Mountains.

Luke squinted, almost losing sight of the huge vessel as the shadows of the undersea cliffs concealed it. But he could still just barely make it out in the darkening waters. It cruised toward a large passageway between two rugged underwater cliffs.

"There are no Whaladons this way—destination unknown," said Admiral Ackbar, wondering where Captain Dunwell was headed.

It was a dangerous journey through the jagged mountains that stretched across the bottom of the sea. There were hot currents that bubbled up and shook their Calamarian minisub, and there were falling rocks that tumbled through the water and almost crushed them.

When they finally emerged from a hollow space that formed a natural tunnel in the mountain, they reached a valley unlike any that Luke had ever seen. It was bathed in the soft green light of a luminous, flowery vine forest. Every few moments there were glints of color sparkling through the water, glows from alien eel creatures that lived and thrived in the depths of the Calamarian ocean. He stared in wonder at the eels and at the huge gleaming pearls, hundreds of them, inside the open mouths of the giant oysters on the valley floor.

Luke didn't know what surprised him more—the number of oysters or their size. Any one of them was large enough to swallow him with one quick bite.

But the pearls and slithering eel creatures weren't all that was gleaming. There was a glint from jagged edges that seemed to be scraps of metal.

Artoo's domed top swiveled around and his little radar screen popped up as high as it could go. He tooted and whistled.

"Tweeeeez bziiiiii!"

"Well, I do believe you're correct, Artoo," Threepio exclaimed. "It's like a mine field. There are pieces of metal debris everywhere."

"It looks like something exploded," said Admiral Ackbar. "Luke, can your Artoo unit examine a piece of metal and determine its atomic structure?"

"Jizoookch!" squawked Artoo.

"Affirmative, sir," Threepio explained.

"Let's use the arm-scoop then," said Ackbar.

Skillfully handling the control for the underwater arm-scoop, the admiral extended a long rod that had a metal claw at its end. The claw grabbed a small piece of scrap metal, then the rod was pulled back into their minisub.

In a moment a narrow slot popped open on the floor near Luke's right boot, revealing the piece of metal that the arm-scoop had just pulled out of the ocean.

Luke reached for it. "Here you go, Artoo," he said, holding it in front of his little utility droid. "Take a quick reading on this."

"I'm especially interested to know whether it contains any doonium or phobium," said Ackbar.

"*Gooooo-zizzz beee-zeeez!*" beeped Artoo.

Threepio translated Artoo's answer. The metal was six percent doonium, a very heavy element used by the Empire in most of its war machines. The metal was also three percent phobium.

"Phobium was mined by Emperor Palpatine on Gargon," said Ackbar. "And there's only one thing I know of that he ever used it for: to coat the power core of the Death Star."

Luke's eyes widened in astonishment. "So then these are scraps from the power core of the exploded Death Star!" He stared through the front porthole again. The Whaladon-hunting submarine had stopped.

A small sub that Luke guessed was an emergency-escape vehicle exited the Whaladon-hunting submarine. But now it was being used for exploration, not for escape.

Slowly and steadily it approached a large chunk of twisted scrap metal, one almost as large as an Imperial command speeder. Luke felt a shiver run up his spine as he suddenly realized what was about to happen.

CHAPTER 6
Ten Minutes to Self-Destruct

A hatch on the escape sub opened and Trioculus emerged alone, while Grand Moff Hissa and the others remained behind.

Trioculus wore a diving suit of the most advanced design, equipped with a helmet that had a miniature arc light. He took a supply of thermal detonators with him.

KABRAAAA-AAM!

The thermal detonators blasted a hole in the side of the large chunk of the Death Star sprawled across the ocean floor. Then Trioculus pulled himself through the hole into the big, hollow piece of metallic debris. He adjusted the arc light on his helmet so that he could examine the crushed mechanical parts that surrounded him.

He found a large lump that looked like the remains of a melted energy dish. He also found a maze of mashed turbolaser cooling tubes and ion equalizers, scorched and clumped together so that they were almost unrecognizable.

And then his third eye noticed three black fingertips sticking out from beneath a mashed ion deactivator.

He pushed aside the ion deactivator, and there it was: a five-fingered black gauntlet, in one piece, undamaged by heat or water.

In fact, the glove looked just as it must have looked when Darth Vader had worn it on his right hand!

Luke bit his lower lip as he kept staring through the front porthole of the Calamarian minisub. Using underwater macrobinoculars, he could see that the diver had three eyes—Trioculus! The Imperial tyrant was reentering the escape sub, and Luke wondered whether Trioculus had just found the glove of Darth Vader.

"Ackbar, can we catch up with that little sub before it gets back inside the Whaladon-hunting submarine?" Luke asked.

"I don't see how," Ackbar replied somberly. "If we get too close, we'll be discovered. One blast from their laser cannons and we'll be finished."

"I say it's time to retreat then," said Threepio.

Luke remembered the words of Yoda, his Jedi teacher: *Luke, the coming fight is yours alone. There is no avoiding the battle—you cannot escape your destiny.*

"We're not going to retreat, Threepio," said Luke. He turned to the Calamarian fishman beside him. "Admiral Ackbar, is there any way we could signal Trioculus and communicate with him somehow?"

"You mean let him know that we're here?"

"Exactly. If we surrender to him, then he'll take us aboard to question us, right? But that will be the biggest mistake he'll ever make."

"Or the biggest one *we'll* ever make," said Ackbar.

Another thought struck Luke. "The other thing we could do is attack."

"Attack!" exclaimed Threepio.

It was an old Jedi rule of thumb to attack when the odds were overwhelmingly against you, and when there was no other possible way to save your own life or the life of an ally. Luke had used that strategy aboard Jabba the Hutt's skiff when Luke and his friends were about to be executed.

"Ackbar, let's get closer to them," said Luke. "Full speed ahead."

"Full speed ahead," repeated Admiral Ackbar reluctantly.

"Oh, dear, I do hope you know what you're doing, Master Luke," said Threepio in a whining voice. "Don't say I didn't warn you—"

Admiral Ackbar pushed hard on the overdrive booster, making their Calamarian minisub go at maximum speed.

FAZHOOOOM!

Their sub lurched forward in the water, then the power suddenly failed. It was totally dark.

"I tried to accelerate faster than we can go, triggering a systems shutdown," said Ackbar. "Threepio, reach up and put your hand on the emergency control lever just above your head. And yank hard."

Threepio did as he was told. The backup generator turned on, and an emergency steering unit popped out of the ceiling, practically landing in Threepio's lap.

"Just push up on that red knob, Threepio," Ackbar continued.

"Pushing as instructed," said Threepio. "Oh, dear."

"Now just hold it steady and steer us on a straight course. The main pilot control should automatically switch on again in about one minute."

"But I haven't the faintest idea how to pilot this thing," Threepio protested.

"It's easy, even a housekeeping droid could do it," said Ackbar. "Just hold that red knob steady."

Threepio tried his best, but the Calamarian minisub tilted on its side, then flipped upside down and plunged straight for the bottom. Then, just seconds before it was about to smash on some rocks, he pulled it out of its nosedive.

"*Bzeeech! Chnoooch!*" beeped Artoo frantically.

"Well, you try to steer it, then, if you think you're so smart," said Threepio. "Hmmph. 'Even a housekeeping droid could do it'!"

At that moment the main pilot control switched back on and Admiral Ackbar took over once again.

"If I could make a suggestion, Master Luke," said Threepio, "I *really* think we ought to head back. We can return to see the sights down here some other time."

"*Zgoonukooo!*" squealed Artoo.

"Yikes!" shouted Threepio. "A giant squid!"

He was right. Luke glanced out the front port-hole and saw a squid larger than any he could ever have imagined. It had long, writhing, twisting tentacles with big, grotesque suction cups. The squid jetted through the water just overhead and passed them.

Suddenly the Whaladon-hunting submarine created another whirlpool, which churned like an angry tornado, going right toward the squid.

FWISHHHHH!

The squid was caught in the whirlpool, but then so was the Calamarian minisub! Around and around they spun, tumbling and falling as they felt the whirlpool sucking them through the opening of a storage chamber right along with the giant squid.

"Oh, nooooo!" shouted Threepio. "Master Luke, we're dooooomed!"

* * *

No one aboard the Whaladon-hunting submarine even realized that the Calamarian minisub had been sucked into the hold along with the giant squid.

The crew members were more concerned with a game that had just begun, a gambling game known as sabacc. Sabacc was a card game that had become very popular in the casinos of Cloud City on Bespin, and now it was played by both humans and aliens on dozens of planets.

A few Aqualish with big tusks began the game, and soon they were joined by others, as they crouched in the main corridor not far from the decompression chamber.

But the game wasn't going smoothly. The Aqualish began growling and pushing, calling each other cheaters and opening their mouths, flashing their teeth and tusks, even spitting at one another.

Trioculus, whose body had just returned to its normal pressure, came out of the decompression chamber. With his black uniform properly in place again, he turned his attention to the glove of Darth Vader.

The droid Emdee had cleaned away the grime and then brought the black glove back to his master, whose right hand trembled as he reached for it. Trioculus put the glove on slowly, regally, like a king setting a crown on his head. An image of Darth Vader flashed into Trioculus's mind, and at that instant the evil of Vader seemed to pour through him like a sudden surge of power from the Dark Side.

"It fits your hand perfectly, your lordship," said Grand Moff Hissa, flattering Trioculus, "as though it were made for you to wear!"

They proceeded to Captain Dunwell's cabin.

When they approached the part of the corridor where the sabacc game was being played, Grand Moff Hissa cautioned Trioculus, telling him that the noisy Aqualish gamblers in their path seemed to be out of control.

As Trioculus drew closer, the gang of Aqualish didn't even look up, let alone step out of his way. They were as rude and stupid as any Aqualish he had ever encountered anywhere in the galaxy.

Grand Moff Hissa clicked his heels to get their attention. "Why aren't you Aqualish at your work stations?" he demanded.

But there was no reply, only a snarling growl from the loser and a coarse laugh from the winner as he picked up his credit chips. Trioculus's three eyes turned fiery.

"You are blocking the path of the Supreme Ruler of the Empire!" Grand Moff Hissa shouted. "Clear a path and get back to work now or you'll all be executed!"

The one with the thickest tusks just sneered, then spit on the floor and hissed at the Imperials.

"How dare you!" an enraged Trioculus boomed, raising the glove of Darth Vader and pointing it at the Aqualish who had just insulted him.

But to Trioculus's amazement nothing happened.

The glove didn't work for him the way it had worked for Darth Vader, who had been able to choke the life-breath out of his victims by pointing the glove in their direction.

Scowling, Trioculus raised his other hand and lightning bolts flowed from his fingertips, causing the offending Aqualish to crumple to the ground, kicking and writhing. The electricity quickly reduced him to an unrecognizable heap.

The remaining Aqualish scattered at once, without any further incident. Moments later Trioculus, Grand Moff Hissa, and Emdee arrived at the captain's private quarters.

Captain Dunwell agreed to depart so that the Imperial leader could confer with his most trusted advisors without being disturbed.

Shaking his head in disgust, Trioculus sat down in the captain's favorite chair. "When Darth Vader pointed this glove, he had the power to choke his victims," he said. "The glove is useless if it no longer has that power."

"The important thing to remember," said Grand Moff Hissa, "is that the glove is a great symbol of evil. As we know, the Supreme Prophet of the Dark Side, Kadann, prophesied that the new Emperor would wear that glove. And now that you wear it, none of the Imperial warlords can question your claim to be our new Emperor. And Kadann won't be able to question your authority, either, once we go to Space Station Scardia and prove to him that you have found it."

"I'm not interested in *symbols*," said Trioculus. "I want the same power as Darth Vader!"

Grand Moff Hissa continued. "My lord, you must realize that, though you are a great slavelord, it could still take many years for you to become a True Master of the Dark Side. Don't forget, the lightning bolts don't flow naturally from your fingertips like they did with Emperor Palpatine. Emdee had to implant a cybernetic device inside of you so that you could appear to have the lightning power. But if you use it too many times, all that electricity could prove fatal to you. You mustn't use it anymore. Fortunately, however, the lightning device has already served its purpose. It helped us to convince everyone that you *are* the Emperor's son, which is exactly what the Central Committee of Grand Moffs wanted to do."

"Never forget," Trioculus said with a blaze of anger in all three of his eyes, "that when the Central Committee of Grand Moffs proposed to me that I be the one to declare himself the Emperor's son, you grand moffs swore you would keep the plot a secret. And in turn I agreed that when I became Emperor, I would share my rule with the Central Committee of Grand Moffs."

"And I hope *you* shall never forget," said Grand Moff Hissa, bearing his pointy teeth, "that we dreamed up this plot only because we had absolutely no choice. The Emperor's real three-eyed son, Triclops, is hopelessly insane, and all of our attempts to cure him have met with failure. Obviously it's better that a trusted three-eyed mutant, such as yourself, should take his place, my lord. If we were to permit Triclops to rule the Empire, his madness would surely bring about the end of us all!"

Emdee removed a small utility case from his left side. He opened the case, then carefully took out five very tiny mechanisms, each the size of a man's fingertip.

"I can put one of these inside the tip of each of the glove's fingers," Emdee said, holding one of them up. "When your fingers press against these devices, they will give off a piercing, high-frequency sound, an earsplitting pitch heard only by the one you've aimed the glove at. It will make your victims gasp and fall to their knees. Their eardrums will explode and their brains disintegrate, just like Darth Vader was able to do with his own natural power."

* * *

Luke stared through a minisub window down at the giant squid, which lay almost lifeless in a huge, cube-shaped Whaladon storage chamber. He breathed a sigh of relief that the squid had been stunned into a state of unconsciousness by the whirlpool. However, there was no relief at all for him when he realized that the minisub was trapped inside the same storage chamber as the squid. Although Luke, Admiral Ackbar, and the two droids were safe for the moment, they had to find a way out—fast.

Ackbar piloted their minisub to the top of the storage chamber, which was filled with seawater. Then he attached their sub magnetically to a hatch that led into the main corridor of the Whaladon-hunting submarine. Artoo sent an electronic signal that caused the hatch to pop open.

"Good work, Artoo," said Luke. "Admiral Ackbar, I think you should wait here and be ready in case we need to make a quick escape."

Moments later Luke, Artoo, and Threepio walked cautiously down the corridor. Passing several other Whaladon storage chambers, they looked down into them and saw a trapped Whaladon in each.

Then they saw the chamber where Leviathor was imprisoned. Leviathor was flapping his tail aimlessly, moaning sadly.

Luke spied Captain Dunwell, who was standing alone, armed with a standard blaster, staring down at Leviathor. Luke recognized Dunwell immediately from the WANTED holograms that Ackbar had projected for him.

The captain was stroking his beard. He was deeply disturbed because he had overheard the conversation between Trioculus, Grand Moff Hissa, and Emdee. Captain Dunwell had deliberately bugged his own quarters with hidden microphones. And Trioculus, in his haste to find a private place to talk, had forgotten to have Grand Moff Hissa check for any listening devices.

The captain now knew some very dark and dangerous secrets. But what should he do with this information?

As Captain Dunwell glanced up, he suddenly noticed Luke, Threepio, and Artoo. He pulled out his blaster and fired two short blasts, one of which struck Artoo and sent the little droid spinning around and around in a circle.

Luke instantly drew his lightsaber. He struck the

blade against Captain Dunwell's blaster, and the weapon tumbled out of the captain's hand.

"Who are you?" the captain demanded. "And how did you get on board this ship?"

"I'm asking the questions and giving the orders now, Captain," said Luke. "And here's order number one. You're going to find us a computer terminal so we can hook up with this ship's master control system."

"A computer terminal won't do you any good," replied the captain. "You could *never* decipher our data codes."

"I seriously doubt that Artoo here will have any problem with your codes," said Luke.

"Kill me if you want. But I'll never help you!"

Using a Jedi mind trick that Obi-Wan Kenobi had taught him, Luke looked Captain Dunwell straight in the eyes and said, "You've mistaken us for your enemies."

"I've mistaken you for my enemies," a dazed Captain Dunwell repeated in a soft voice.

"You wanted us to come here so we could help you."

"I wanted you to come here," said the captain.

"We're supposed to check your master control," said Luke, continuing to use his Jedi mind power. "Now take us to a computer terminal quickly."

"I will take you to a terminal."

The captain lead them up one corridor and down another. Finally he showed them to a computer terminal.

"Artoo," said Luke, "hook into this terminal and figure out how to crack the communication code. Then instruct the ship's master control to open the doors to the Whaladon storage chambers. Let all the Whaladons free!"

Artoo extended a little metal arm and hooked himself into the computer terminal.

"You fool," said Captain Dunwell, recovering his senses. "You think that little utility droid of yours can crack a code I spent three years creating?"

"*Gaaaaaz booop dweeet!*" beeped Artoo.

"He says you underestimate him, Captain," said Threepio. "He says Darth Vader's codes used to be *much* more complicated than yours, and it never took him more than fifteen seconds to figure *those* out."

"Artoo, I just thought of something," Luke said. "Before you free the Whaladons, the first thing you should do is scan the ship's data banks. Find out if this vessel has a self-destruct system."

"It doesn't," said Captain Dunwell.

"*Zuuuuung! Galooooop!*" squawked Artoo.

"Artoo says it does, Master Luke," Threepio confirmed.

"Excellent," said Luke. "Find out the precise self-destruct code. Tell me when you've got it."

"Trioculus expects me to be back in the navigation room by now," said Captain Dunwell. "If he comes looking for me and finds you, he'll destroy you instantly!"

"*Zoooosh-bee-dwee,*" beeped Artoo, rolling his

domed top around to show his excitement.

"He has the self-destruct code, Master Luke," explained Threepio.

"Good droid, Artoo. Now punch in the self-destruct code and set the ship to blow up in . . . "

Luke stopped to think. How much time would the Whaladons need to swim to a safe distance? And how much time would he, his droids, and Admiral Ackbar need to get their Calamarian minisub away from here without being destroyed by a gigantic explosion?

"Give us ten minutes—that should do .it," said Luke. "And if it doesn't, well then we're all history."

"You can't do this!" Captain Dunwell protested.

Artoo beeped and squeaked and whirred. *"Booooshsh! Zweeech!"*

"Artoo says yes we can," Threepio translated. "Just watch us."

"Ziiish bajoooop!" Artoo tooted.

"Self-destruct is activated, Master Luke!" reported Threepio.

Just then alarm bells started to go off and warning lights blinked along the corridor.

CHAPTER 7
The Captain's Reward

"Quick, Artoo!" said Luke. "Tell the master control to free the Whaladons!"

"He's searching for a way to do it, Master Luke," said Threepio. "He's looking and—oh, gracious, he can't find it! Keep looking, Artoo. We've got to save Leviathor and the other Whaladons before—"

Suddenly Trioculus appeared down at the end of the hall. "Oh, no, Master Luke, Trioculus has found us!" Threepio shouted. "We're doomed!"

"Your droid has grasped your situation well, Skywalker," said Trioculus. He raised his gloved right hand and pointed it at Luke. "Now prepare to die!" he shouted.

Luke ducked behind Captain Dunwell. Gripping the captain, Luke positioned him directly in front of the glove of Darth Vader.

Captain Dunwell gasped as a high-pitched deadly sound vibration struck him. Luke then lifted the captain and heaved him, making him collide with Trioculus and toppling them both to the floor. Then Luke drew out his lightsaber.

"*Jeeep booo poooooz!*" tooted Artoo.

"Success!" shouted Threepio. "Artoo has instructed the master control to free the Whaladons!"

Just then the doors of the Whaladon storage chambers began to open. All the while the alarm bells were getting louder and the warning lights were flashing faster. Time was getting short before the Whaladon-hunting submarine would self-destruct in a furious explosion that would destroy them all.

Trioculus raised his left hand, electricity crackling from his fingertips. Luke met the electric bolt with his lightsaber, deflecting it. Trioculus's eyes bulged and his chest froze, as the warning of Grand Moff Hissa flooded back into his mind. The lightning power would be the death of him if he continued to use it. He was not yet a True Master of the Dark Side, not yet able to absorb intense electric shock without experiencing side effects.

But Trioculus allowed the flow of electricity to increase, aiming the bolts so that they would avoid Luke's lightsaber blade and strike him directly in the chest.

Luke crumpled to the ground, writhing on the floor as he felt the full force of the powerful jolts. Trioculus continued to pour bolts of electricity from his fingertips until Luke had stopped stirring. Then he lowered his hand and spoke rapidly into a pocket communication device. "Hissa, power up the escape sub! Quickly!"

Hissa's reply came from the device. "We'll need Captain Dunwell's key card to power it up!"

Trioculus turned to the captain. "Hand me your key card for the escape sub! At once!"

By the time Trioculus had snatched the key card from Captain Dunwell's hand, Luke Skywalker was back on his feet and was running down the corridor that would lead him to the Calamarian minisub.

"You may have escaped from Emperor Palpatine, but I shall destroy you, Skywalker!" Trioculus shouted. "You have my promise!"

Luke kept running—all the way back to the Calamarian minisub. He crawled through the hatch and saw that Threepio and Admiral Ackbar were already strapped into their seats waiting for him, and Artoo was in position, too.

They began their escape. The giant squid was just beginning to stir as Ackbar deftly navigated their Calamarian minisub over its slowly writhing body. A

tentacle nearly grabbed them, but Ackbar success-
fully steered a course through the open door of the
storage chamber and into the ocean depths.

As they sailed away, Luke looked out the window and saw Leviathor leading the freed Whaladons
back through the Seascape Mountains, swimming as
fast as their fins would take them.

Trioculus reached the escape sub with only two
minutes remaining until the self-destruct system
would blast the Whaladon-hunting submarine apart.
Emdee and Grand Moff Hissa were waiting for him.
Captain Dunwell arrived breathless seconds later.

"Let me get aboard first so I can warm up the ion
thrusters," said the captain as Trioculus inserted the
key card into the lock of the escape sub's door.

"Just a moment," replied Grand Moff Hissa,
standing in his way. "No one enters the escape sub
before the Supreme Ruler of the Empire, the True
Master of the Dark Side."

Captain Dunwell turned to face Trioculus. "And
are you the True Master of the Dark Side?" said Captain Dunwell without thinking. "I thought a Master
of the Dark Side didn't need to rely on mechanical
devices to give him lightning power or to make the
glove of Darth—"

He stopped in mid-sentence, his face turning
pale as he realized he had said too much about things
he wasn't supposed to know.

"Out of my way," snapped Trioculus, glaring at
the captain.

As Trioculus began to climb into the escape sub, he felt a stabbing pain in his eyes. For a second everything went black, but then he pressed his forehead, blinked a few times, and the momentary loss of vision went away. He could see again, and he hastily strapped himself into a seat.

Grand Moff Hissa climbed in, too, followed by Emdee.

But when Captain Dunwell tried to join them, the Imperial ruler stared at him with a piercing hypnotic glare and said calmly, "You know the procedure, Captain. In the Empire the captain always goes down with his ship."

"Lord Trioculus, I led you to the glove of Darth Vader!" said Captain Dunwell, nervously tweaking his beard. "I thought you would show some appreciation. Is death to be my reward?"

"I don't reward men who spy on me, Captain."

"Lord Trioculus, please have mercy, let me aboard— "

As Trioculus pointed the glove of Darth Vadar at him, Captain Dunwell tried to shut out the piercing sound that suddenly assaulted his eardrums. The captain's eyes then twirled upward as he let out a hoarse gasp, fell to his knees, and then dropped to the floor.

Hissa kicked the door shut and locked it. Leaving Captain Dunwell behind to die with his crew, the escape sub pushed away from the Whaladon-hunting submarine, making its way higher in the ocean as it sailed toward the dim outline of the undersea mountain range.

Moments later the escape sub shook violently as a tremendous explosion tore apart the Whaladon-hunting submarine, sending scraps of scorched metal spinning through the sea in all directions.

An evil smile spread across Trioculus's face as he clenched his gloved right hand into a fist. That hand no longer twitched. It now felt strong, invincible—and ready to rule the galaxy!

Luke's adventure had led him back to the place where it all began—on Yavin Four, where Luke and his droids were now gathered in the Alliance Senate. They had just finished delivering a complete report to SPIN on all that they had accomplished on their mission.

Luke, Threepio, and Artoo were congratulated by SPIN, not just for their espionage on Kessel but for their help in saving the Whaladons.

When the meeting had adjourned and most of the SPIN members departed, Admiral Ackbar turned to Luke, Threepio, Artoo, and Princess Leia and said, "On behalf of the planet Calamari, as a special thanks, I'd like to invite you all to be our guests of honor at a special concert of Whaladon songs at our Domed City of Aquarius."

"*Fzzzzoooop bedoooooop!*" squeaked Artoo in a scolding tone.

"I'm very sorry to report," Threepio said in a disappointed voice, "that Artoo absolutely *refuses*

ever to return to Calamari with me again—that is, until I get a license to steer a Calamarian minisub!"

Luke laughed, remembering that Threepio's brief moments of piloting the minisub had almost been the death of them. However, with a little coaxing from Luke, Artoo was persuaded to change his mind.

Sure enough, when the day of the Whaladon concert arrived, Luke and his friends were once again on Calamari, seated in the aquatheater in the Domed City of Aquarius.

The program of Whaladon songs was spectacular. It included a water ballet, Whaladon folk melodies, classical Whaladon songs, and an opera Leviathor had composed that told the legendary story of how he had become the Whaladon leader many years ago by helping the Whaladons survive an undersea volcanic eruption.

As much as Luke enjoyed the concert, being back on Calamari made him think about those final fateful moments before the Whaladon-hunting submarine had exploded, when he had glanced back and noticed the Imperial escape sub departing.

Had that escape sub been destroyed by the hurtling debris? Or had Trioculus survived, making it back to the planet's watery surface so that he could live to fight another day?

Try as he might to forget the Imperial leader's dire threat, Luke was unable to banish from his mind Trioculus's parting words: *"I shall destroy you, Skywalker! You have my promise!"*

Glossary

Admiral Ackbar
Rebel military leader, he is a fishman from the planet Calamari.

Aqualish aliens
Walrus-faced, with smooth skin and large eyes, Aqualish aliens have nasty dispositions. They live on watery planets, and turn their natural aggressions toward all aliens other than their own kind.

Artoo-Detoo (R2-D2)
A barrel-shaped utility droid belonging to Luke Skywalker. Artoo cannot speak in words, but communicates in beeps, buzzes, and whistles that are translated by his companion, See-Threepio (C-3PO). An effective copilot and troubleshooter, Artoo can rapidly penetrate the data system of almost any computer in the galaxy.

Calamarian minisub
A small submarine that Luke, Admiral Ackbar, Threepio, and Artoo use to follow and spy on the huge Whaladon-hunting submarine.

Captain Dunwell
The crazed human captain of the Whaladon-hunting submarine. He wears a blue uniform with medals

and has a neatly trimmed white beard that he likes to tweak.

His great goal is to capture Leviathor, leader of the Whaladons. He has tried to trap Leviathor for many years, throughout the Great War, but every time Leviathor has avoided capture.

Chewbacca

A hairy, eight-foot-tall, 205-year-old Wookiee who serves as copilot aboard the *Millennium Falcon*. Chewbacca (also known as Chewie) uses his strength to assist the Rebel Alliance, usually serving alongside his buddy Han Solo.

Darth Vader

Now deceased, Darth Vader was the second-in-command of the Galactic Empire, serving under the evil Emperor Palpatine. He was born as Annakin Skywalker and was Luke and Leia's father, but he turned to the Dark Side of the Force and tried unsuccessfully to convince Luke to join the Empire. More machine than man, Darth Vader was kept alive by cybernetic devices—and a breathing apparatus built into his black helmet.

Doonium

A heavy metal used by the Empire in most of its war machines.

Domed City of Aquarius

This domed city is located inside a giant bubble under the ocean on the planet Calamari. It was designed for both creatures with lungs and creatures with gills. It has watery canals with underwater dwellings, and above the canals are markets and homes for air-breathers.

Emdee-Five (MD-5)

An evil Imperial droid with a wide variety of skills, including medical knowledge. MD-5 (called Emdee) is usually at Trioculus's side and always does Trioculus's bidding, no matter what the request. Trioculus has a close relationship with Emdee, much like Luke's relationship with his droids.

Emperor Palpatine

Now deceased, Emperor Palpatine was once a senator in the Old Republic, but he destroyed the old democratic order and established the ruthless Galactic Empire in its place. He ruled the galaxy with military might and tyranny, forcing human and alien citizens of every planet to live in fear. He was assisted by Darth Vader, who eventually turned against him, hurling the Emperor to his death in the power core of the Death Star.

Glove of Darth Vader

The glove of Darth Vader's right hand that was cut off by Luke Skywalker in their final battle.

Grand Moff Dunhausen

A grand moff (high-ranking Imperial governor) who wears earrings shaped like laser pistols, he is lean and very crafty.

Grand Moff Hissa

The grand moff whom Trioculus trusts the most. He has spear-pointed teeth.

Grand Moff Muzzer
A grand moff who is plump and round-faced, he is brash and excitable.

Grand Moff Thistleborn
A grand moff with bushy eyebrows, he is authoritative and very loyal to the Central Committee of Grand Moffs.

Han Solo
A Corellian cargo pilot whose spaceship, the *Millennium Falcon*, served the Rebel Alliance in the fight against the Imperial Death Star. Han is a freewheeling, independent-minded bachelor who usually travels with his Wookiee companion, Chewbacca—but he does have a soft spot for Princess Leia.

Imperial minisub
Attached to the Whaladon-hunting submarine, this is a small probe sub that can seat four or five people. It also serves as an escape sub in the event of an emergency.

Leviathor
The leader of the Whaladons, he is the ancient one who knows the entire history of his species. He is a wise and great ruler, and his leadership has helped many Whaladons to remain free by outsmarting the Whaladon hunters.

Leviathor is a white Whaladon—the only great white still alive.

Luke Skywalker
A Jedi Knight from Tatooine, now a Commander in the Rebel Alliance. Luke was trained in the secret knowledge

of the Force by Obi-Wan Kenobi and Yoda. Princess Leia is his twin sister.

Mon Mothma
A distinguished-looking leader, she has long been in charge of the Rebel Alliance.

Obi-Wan Kenobi
Obi-Wan Kenobi was a Jedi Master who taught Luke Skywalker to use the Force. Obi-Wan passed away when he was defeated by Darth Vader in a lightsaber duel, but he is still sometimes seen by Luke in dreams and visions.

Phobium
A metal that Emperor Palpatine used to coat the power core of the Death Star.

Princess Leia Organa
Raised by a senator of the Old Republic on Alderaan, a planet that was destroyed by the Empire, Princess Leia is Luke Skywalker's twin sister. Courageous and outspoken, she is a valuable member of the Rebel Alliance in its fight against Imperial forces.

See-Threepio (C-3PO)
A golden, human-shaped protocol droid belonging to Luke Skywalker, See-Threepio can translate six million galactic languages and is an expert at droid-human relations. He is seldom seen without his sidekick, Artoo-Detoo (R2-D2).

Trioculus (pronounced *Try-ock-you-luss*)
Supreme Slavelord of the spice mines of the planet Kessel.
After the death of Emperor Palpatine, he comes forward
announcing that he is the Emperor's banished son. He is
a handsome but evil mutant with three eyes, including an
evil eye on his forehead that has hypnotic powers.

Valley of the Giant Oysters
An undersea valley on the planet Calamari that has been
the home of the giant oysters for millions of years.

Whaladons
Whale-like mammals that live underwater on Calamari,
the water world that is the home of the respected Rebel,
Admiral Ackbar, a fishman. Led by the white Whaladon
Leviathor, Whaladons resemble humpback whales but
have a few variations.

Whaladon hunters
Walrus-faced Aqualish aliens who serve under Captain
Dunwell on the Whaladon-hunting submarine.

Whaladon-hunting submarine
This terrifying vessel is as big as an Imperial space battle
cruiser or a small city. Its job is to stun Whaladons and
then suck them into the many on-board storage chambers.
This submarine can store more than a dozen Whaladons
at one time.

Whaladon Processing Center
This is a bleak Imperial installation inside an undersea
crater. Here the bodies of Whaladons are stripped of their

meat and blubber, then loaded into Imperial cargo space-ships to be shipped to places where it is needed.

Yoda

The Jedi Master Yoda was a small creature who lived on the bog planet Dagobah. For eight hundred years before passing away he taught Jedi Knights, including Obi-Wan Kenobi and Luke Skywalker.

THE LOST CITY OF THE JEDI

PAUL DAVIDS
AND HOLLACE DAVIDS

Illustrated by Karl Kesel

The Rebel Alliance

Luke Skywalker

Princess Leia

Han Solo

HC-100

Ken

Chip

Dee-Jay (DJ-88)

Baji

The Empire

Trioculus

Grand Moff Hissa

Emdee-Five (MD-5)

Grand Moff Dunhausen

High Prophet Jedgar

Commodore Zuggs

Supreme Prophet Kadann

Triclops

To our parents,
Cecelia and Frank Goodman,
and Frances and Jules Davids,
May Yoda's wisdom grace you always...

CHAPTER 1
The Bomb and the Dream

As Luke Skywalker knocked on the door of Han Solo's warehouse, a lens popped out of the metal wall, making a curious noise as it examined Luke's face.

BJEE-DITZZZ! BJEE-DITZZZ!

"Please show your galactic ID card and stick out your hand for a fingerprint check," an electronic voice called out.

"Gracious," exclaimed See-Threepio, Luke's golden droid. "Han has certainly become strict about security!"

Artoo-Detoo whistled timidly in agreement.

"Maybe that's because Han's warehouse is in Port Town," replied Luke. "This happens to be one of the most dangerous neighborhoods in Cloud City— a hangout for all types of alien hoods and sleazy, small-time gamblers."

Luke stuck his left hand into the slot, since his right hand was artificial and didn't have any fingerprints. It was mechanical, a replacement for his real right hand, which he lost in a lightsaber duel with the evil Darth Vader.

ZHOOOOOM! The door made a loud sound as it lifted up, allowing Luke and his droids to enter the warehouse.

Chewbacca, the Wookiee, greeted Luke with a friendly squeeze. "Rooow-rowf," he growled.

"Easy there, Chewie, not too hard," said Luke. "I've got a bruised shoulder."

Luke, Threepio, and Artoo had come to the planet Bespin on a mission for SPIN—the Senate Planetary Intelligence Network. Lando Calrissian, the governor of Cloud City, had requested their help because food pirates had invaded all of the big hotels and food storage companies. In the raids stolen food was shipped off to a secret Imperial base for the Empire, who needed food for its army of stormtroopers.

Artoo-Detoo had helped design a Warning and Detection Device—a WADD—to protect the food warehouses. It was an infinitely more sophisticated security system than the old, somewhat primitive device that protected Han's rented warehouse. Luke and his droids had just finished installing a network of delicate WADD units, and since they were in the neighborhood, they decided to drop in on Han.

"*ChNOOOOg-bzeeep*," tooted Artoo to Chewbacca. "*KROOOpch shbeeek znooob pvOOOM!*"

"Artoo would like to point out," Threepio translated, "that Master Luke's shoulder was bruised when we helped the Cloud Police capture a gang of Imperial food pirates—all of them on Cloud City's *Most Wanted* List. One of those nasty rogues kicked Master Luke in the shoulder, causing the skin tissue to turn blue and black."

"We usually refer to it as black and blue," Luke put in, as he rubbed his sore shoulder. "Hey, you ol'

Wookiee," he said, turning to Chewbacca, "are you taking good care of my friend Han?"

"Graaawrrr," roared Chewbacca, indicating that Han was being well cared for.

"Hey, kiddo," said Han, peeking out from underneath his unfinished house, his hands filled with tools. The house was floating in the air, about three feet above the warehouse floor. Han dusted himself off and stepped out to greet his friend. "How's Her Royal Highness, Princess Leia?"

"She misses you," Luke said.

"She does?" Han asked with a hint of excitement in his voice. "I thought she was so mad at me for going off to build my sky house, that she'd have forgotten me by now."

Luke shook his head. "She misses you quite a lot, in fact. When you said good-bye to leave for the Kessel mission, she. . ." Luke stopped himself in midsentence, glancing around in sudden amazement. "Wow! I didn't know that you were building a mansion, Han."

"A floating mansion," Han said, laughing.

Han took Luke on a little walk around the outside of the house, pointing out all of its special features.

"I've been from one end of this galaxy to the other," said Han, his voice swelling with pride, "and I've never seen another house like this one. It's a new concept of mine—houses that float in the sky. If you don't like the cloud you're living on, you just drift off to another one."

"Rowww-Roofff!" growled Chewbacca. The

Wookiee turned a repulsorlift control knob, causing the house to lower smoothly and gently to the floor.

"Chewie wants to show off the floor plan, so step right inside," Han said.

Luke couldn't believe his eyes. Han's house had outdoor observation decks, a big kitchen under a transparent dome, lots of bedrooms with floating beds, a circular living room that could be turned to face any direction, a workroom for building everything from blasters to airspeeders, a two-cloud-car garage, and—

"Impressed?" Han asked with a wide grin.

Luke smiled and nodded.

"Very impressive," said Threepio. "What do you think, Artoo?"

"*Chziiiich!*" Artoo tooted enthusiastically, indicating that he was very impressed indeed.

"I was just wondering, Han," said Luke, "is there any special reason why you made the house with so many bedrooms?"

"Why do you ask?" Han replied suspiciously.

Luke gave a shy smile. "Well, I guess I was just wondering if you ever intend to get married and fill this house with kids."

Han laughed. "Who, me? Give up my bachelor ways and settle down? That's a real long shot, if ever I heard one." Han scratched his chin, giving Luke's question a little thought. "Of course," he went on, "I suppose I'd have to admit that there's always one chance in a hundred that it could happen."

Luke looked his old friend straight in the eye.

"Come on, Han," he said, "you can tell me. Were you thinking about marrying my sister Leia when you built this huge place?"

Han just laughed. "If I ever do decide to get married, which is *highly* improbable, Leia is at the top of my list. But this is all just wild speculation."

"Very wild speculation, I'm sure," Luke said, nodding. But the truth was, he wasn't so sure.

Han changed the subject by putting on a chef's apron and cooking them a spicy Corellian meal on his new nanowave stove. The hot and saucy dish was a favorite back on Han's home planet. Chewie then demonstrated his newfound cooking abilities by serving up one of his zoochberry pies for dessert.

"Congratulations, Chewie," Luke said, patting his full belly when they were done eating. "That was about the best zoochberry pie I've ever had! I wish we could stay longer, but we've got to return to Yavin Four now and get back to SPIN headquarters."

Han and Chewie accompanied Luke, Threepio, and Artoo to the hangar where Luke had parked his Y-wing starfighter spaceship. "Are you sure I can't talk you into coming back to Yavin Four with me?" Luke asked Han. "SPIN could sure use your help."

"I'll pass," Han replied. "All I want to do now is complete *my* mission—which is finishing my sky house."

The two buddies said their farewells, and after the two droids were aboard, Luke shut the door to his Y-wing starfighter. He strapped himself into the pilot's seat, waiting long enough for Han and Chewbacca to move a safe distance away from the ship.

Luke pressed the power button, only nothing happened except—

KLIK-KLIK-KLIK . . .

The clicking sound kept growing louder and louder. Luke leaned forward to check the switch.

"Careful, Master Luke," Threepio said, "that sound might mean that—"

But before Threepio could finish his sentence, a sudden explosion hurled Luke back in his chair, so hard that his safety straps tore loose.

BROOOOMMPF!

Luke flipped over backward, knocking his head against the floor. The blast hurled the thruster into his right arm, tearing open his mechanical hand.

The interior of the spaceship was in shambles. Flames were spreading, filling the ship with smoke.

Within seconds, Han and Chewbacca burst in-

side to help. Chewbacca and Threepio quickly put out the fire, and Han lifted the thruster, freeing Luke's trapped hand. Then he knelt beside his friend.

"You seem to be in pretty bad shape, kiddo," Han said. "We'd better get you some medical attention."

"Oh, I do hope you'll be okay, Master Luke," said Threepio. "One of the food pirates obviously sent us a nasty farewell present."

"Grrooooof!" moaned Chewbacca, holding up a tiny, charred mechanism he found on the floor.

"Dweeeep dzeeen-boop!" Artoo tooted.

"Yes, yes, Artoo, I know," Threepio replied. "That's a miniature bomb detonator. Manufactured by the Empire!"

Thanks to the help of Lando Calrissian, Luke was transported at once to the Cloud City hospital, where a team of medical droids examined him immediately. The news about his condition was encouraging. Luke had lots of bruises and several cracked ribs, but no broken bones. However, the control unit in his mechanical right hand had been smashed by the spaceship's power booster.

Luke couldn't bend the fingers of his mechanical hand at all. And the hospital didn't have the right spare parts. In fact, not a single medical supply outfit in Cloud City had them. Luke's artificial hand would have to be repaired back on Yavin Four, and delicate surgery was definitely required.

It was obvious to Han that Luke was going to need a pilot and a spaceship to get him back to Yavin's fourth moon. It might take weeks to repair Luke's Y-wing starfighter, and besides, Luke was in no condition to pilot. Han resigned himself that his sky house was going to have to wait. Friendship came first.

With Chewbacca serving as Han's copilot, they departed with Luke and the droids at dawn. The *Millennium Falcon*'s hyperdrive unit was in tip-top condition. At faster-than-light speed, it was the quickest trip Han had ever made from Cloud City to the fourth moon of Yavin. As they made their approach, the moon loomed before them in space, wrapped in the green glow of its luxurious forests.

When Luke awoke from a long nap, Chewbacca was already shutting down the hyperdrive thrusters, and See-Threepio and Artoo-Detoo were preparing for the landing.

The *Millennium Falcon* began a smooth descent toward the main landing bay of Yavin Four. There they were met by Princess Leia.

"Don't worry, your Highness," Han said in a reassuring voice, as Leia led them toward the Senate building. "Luke had a little run-in with an exploding bomb, but fortunately your brother's like a Kowakian lizard-monkey that has nine lives."

"Thanks for bringing him home," Leia said.

"Hey, what are friends for?" Han said, putting an arm around her. He stared deeply into her bright, brown eyes. "Luke said you missed me," he said. "Sorry I've been such a hermit, Princess. I'll make it up to you. I promise."

Han stopped Leia to give her a very long kiss.

And against the Princess's better judgment, she didn't try to make it any shorter.

While Luke lay in bed in the Central Clinic of Yavin Four, recovering from the operation that repaired his mechanical hand, Princess Leia asked his permission to send Threepio and Artoo to the neighboring town of Vornez.

"I want them to examine and help upgrade a new group of protocol droids that arrived from the planet Tatooine," she explained. "The new droids can't speak as many languages as Threepio, and they've never been programmed to translate the beeps of an Artoo unit, either."

"I guess I can survive without Threepio and Artoo for a week or two," he said.

A few days later, when Luke had almost completely recovered, he went home from the Central Clinic to his private hideaway on Yavin Four—a white stone tower, built long ago by a vanished alien race called the Massasi. On this foliage-covered moon, many of the ancient archaeological wonders of the Massasi still stood, reminders of these ancient people and their society.

Luke's bedroom was at the top of the tower, just beneath the turret. Standing by one of the windows, he admired the sweeping view that overlooked the neverending rain forest. As dusk became nightfall, Luke lay on his bed and stared up at the stars. Before he knew it, he was sound asleep.

Soon Luke's sleep became fitful.

In his dream, Luke saw himself on a secret mission, zooming along on his airspeeder. He was close above the treetops of the rain forest—and then suddenly the forest burst into flames, with smoke rising all around him. Luke was coughing, choking, losing control of his airspeeder.

It tumbled down into the burning foliage. Luke fell off, plunging through the vines and thick leaves. He landed with a thud on the forest floor. When he looked up, he saw a circular wall made of blocks of green marble. In the center of the circle was a tubular transport for descending underground.

Luke dreamed that he could see his Jedi Master, Obi-Wan Kenobi, standing at the wall, beckoning him, signaling Luke with a wave of his hand to come closer and enter.

"Luke," said Obi-Wan, "this is the entrance that

leads underground to the Lost City of the Jedi. The entire history of the galaxy and all its worlds is recorded there, protected by the caretaker droids of the city. Your destiny is linked to one who lives down there.

"Memorize this code, Luke," Obi-Wan continued. "Its importance shall soon become clear to you: JE-99-DI-88-FOR-00-CE." Then he began to fade away.

Gasping, Luke suddenly awoke from his dream. Beads of sweat dripped from his forehead. He still felt some pain from his ribs.

It was early morning. Luke climbed out of bed, walked over to the narrow tower window, and looked down at the treetops of the rain forest. He wondered what his dream meant. Since the day when Obi-Wan Kenobi had been cut down by Darth Vader's lightsaber blade, the Jedi Master had appeared to Luke several times in visions. At the moment of his death, Obi-Wan's body had mysteriously vanished, leaving the physical universe for a world unknown.

Obi-Wan Kenobi was a Master of the Force, but now Luke could feel the Force inside himself.

He dressed quickly, walked down the tower stairs, and climbed into his airspeeder.

Soon he was soaring above the rain forest, just like in his dream, thinking about Obi-Wan Kenobi's mysterious words.

Luke flew the airspeeder faster and faster.

He didn't understand why. He didn't know where he was headed.

He just trusted the Force—and kept going.

CHAPTER 2
Ken's Secret Journey

Ken was sound asleep when his pet mooka leapt onto his bed and licked his face, trying to wake him. It was like this *every* morning. When would his mooka learn that boys didn't like to get out of bed in the morning? Especially twelve-year-old boys like Ken who always went to bed late.

"Kshhhhhhhh," the mooka cried. "Kshhhhhhhh."

"Down, Zeebo," Ken said, pushing his mooka away. "Get down. How many times do I have to tell you not to bounce onto my bed in the morning. Do you think I like your feathers getting all over my pillows?"

"Kshhhhhhhh."

"And stop kshhhhing in my ear," Ken added. "You do that every morning too. Just once I wish I could hear the bark of a dog, or the meow of cat, instead of the kshhhhh of a mooka."

Zeebo made a whining sound.

"Oh, c'mon, Zeebo—I didn't mean it." Ken pet his mooka behind one of its four pointy ears. "Don't be jealous. You know I love you. Besides, I've never even seen a cat or a dog—except in pictures in the Jedi Library."

Ken got out of bed and stood on tiptoe to reach his

computer notebook, which had a small data screen designed to help write essays and organize his assignments. Ken kept it behind some supplies on his highest shelf, hidden away so that his Homework Correction Droid, HC-100, wouldn't find it if he came snooping around.

HC-100 resembled a droid Ken had studied about called See-Threepio, a golden, human-shaped droid that belonged to the Jedi Knight Luke Skywalker.

DJ-88, the ancient, very knowledgeable droid who was the caretaker of the library, had custom-designed HC-100 for the specific purpose of correcting and grading Ken's homework assignments.

Ken examined his computer notebook, pressing the keypad to call up a report he was working on called "The Moons of Yavin."

When the words flashed on the data screen, a number flashed up, too: "65."

After the number was the comment: "You can do better than this, Ken. Suggestion: Add more detail about moons one and two."

"Oh no!" exclaimed Ken. "This isn't fair at all, Zeebo. HC obviously snuck into my dome-house, found my computer notebook, and graded my report, even though I didn't even finish it yet! He gave me a 65; that's practically failing! HC is turning into a spy and a nuisance and—and I won't miss him a *bit* when I leave today on my secret journey Topworld."

"Kshhhhhhh. . ." Zeebo whined, jumping into Ken's arms and licking his face affectionately.

"Of course I'll miss you," Ken said. "And I know

you'll miss me. Chip and Dee-Jay would probably miss me, too, if droids could have real feelings."

Ken considered Chip, short for Microchip, his best and only friend. Ken often wished that Chip were a human boy, rather than just a metallic droid who was programmed to act like a boy and keep Ken company.

Dee-Jay, Ken's nickname for his caretaker, DJ-88, was a droid that Ken deeply admired. But Ken didn't really consider Dee-Jay a friend, since he was also his one and only professor. Dee-Jay taught Ken astronomy, ecology, computers, and about fifteen other subjects.

"In a way, Zeebo," Ken said, "it was thanks to Dee-Jay that I finally discovered the code to make the tubular transport leave here and go Topworld. Of course Dee-Jay doesn't know that I know it. I peeked into one of his files—a file he told me was none of my business. I know it was wrong. But I've been waiting all my life to take a journey Topworld, and none of the droids will let me. Just think what it will be like—getting to see the rain forests of Yavin Four, riding a starfighter with the Alliance, and maybe even—"

Suddenly, without even a knock, the door to Ken's dome-house popped open, and Chip hurried in carrying a tube of vaporizing tooth-cleaner and a canister of foam soap.

"A very pleasant wake up to you, Ken," said the boy-shaped silver droid, who had flexible, ribbed arms and legs that could bend in almost any direction. "I see that you've hardly even begun to get ready to go to the library for your lessons with Dee-Jay. I'll have to stop trusting the mooka to wake you up on time."

Ken took the hint and began to get dressed. He took off his silver pajamas and then put on his silver school clothes. He didn't know why, but silver was his favorite color. Maybe it was because of the semitransparent, silvery crystal he always wore around his neck. Or maybe it was because silver was the color of Chip. And Chip had been his droid friend and helper for as long as he could remember.

Chip's clumsy boot-shaped feet clattered as he stepped over to the trickle of water flowing down the back wall. The hot, natural water never stopped flowing into Ken's dome-house. It came from an underground stream, and he used it to wash up every morning.

The boy-droid, who was about the same height as Ken, picked up a bowl and began to fill it.

"You should have vapor-cleaned your teeth and combed your hair half an hour ago!" Chip exclaimed.

Ken ran his fingers through his moppy, light-brown hair. "I happen to like my hair when it's messy," Ken explained. "And I don't think a twelve-year-old boy needs help vapor-cleaning his teeth. Do you?"

"Master Ken, you know very well that I don't think. I follow my program. And my program is quite strict. Wake Ken. Wash Ken. Feed Ken. Tell HC whether or not you've done your homework. And speaking of homework, look out the window, Ken!"

Ken didn't have to look out the window to know

that HC was about to enter through the rounded, arched front door. HC had very distinct footsteps, like a soldier marching, and Ken could always hear him coming from the rhythmic sound of his metallic feet.

Sure enough, HC entered Ken's dome-house, his bright blue metallic eyes taking everything in, and his round, open mouth looking as if he had just been caught by surprise. As soon as HC began talking, he sounded like a sergeant in the Rebel Alliance army.

"Time for homework corrections!" HC-100 declared. "And I certainly hope you've given more attention to your other assignments than you did to your report on the moons of Yavin."

"I wasn't even finished with that report, yet, HC!" Ken protested. "And you snuck in here and graded it already!"

"Excuses, excuses," replied HC. "It looked finished to me!"

"Well it wasn't," Ken insisted. "For your information, I was planning on adding stuff about moons one and two. I wish you'd stop coming into my dome-house when I'm not here and grading my computer notebook before I'm ready."

"You know the rules," said HC. "I'm allowed in here for a surprise homework-check at any time."

HC immediately went over to Ken's desk and found the notebook he was looking for.

"Let's see, for Jedi philosophy you've written an essay on the Force. Well, that's a very worthwhile subject to write an essay about," HC said, nodding his head enthusiastically. "And I see that you've finished your quiz on the history of the Great War against the Empire. You've learned to spell Emperor Palpatine's name correctly. He certainly was a horrible emperor, no doubt about it. The galaxy is better off now that he's dead. And what have we here—hmmmmmm, you've correctly described Darth Vader's role as Emperor Palpatine's second-in-command, but, oh no, you've made a serious mistake in your quiz on the Rebel Alliance. Luke Skywalker didn't pilot the *Millennium Falcon* in the first battle against the Death Star. It was Han Solo, and Chewbacca was his copilot. I thought you knew that, Ken!"

Ken sighed. "I do. I guess I must have been daydreaming."

"Daydreaming?" HC asked, surprised. "About what?"

Ken wondered how much to tell HC about his daydreams. He thought about it, as he slowly ran his forefinger across the crystal he wore around his neck. It was shaped like half a sphere, veined with deep blue lines and attached to a thin, silver chain. Ken had worn that crystal as long as he could remember, since the days before he had been brought to this underground place as a very young child. Ken didn't know who had given it to him. And if any of the droids knew, none of them had ever been willing to answer any questions about it.

"I guess I was daydreaming about actually meeting Luke Skywalker and Han Solo and Chewbacca," Ken said finally. "I wonder what it would be like.

Imagine, flying off with them in the *Millennium Falcon!*"

"Honestly, Master Ken, you worry me sometimes," HC said, shaking his head. "Imagine, a boy of your age, wanting to go gallivanting around the galaxy with the Alliance! Remember what Dee-Jay told you. Down here where we live, there's no evil. But up there, Topworld, the spies of the Empire are everywhere, and the Dark Side is strong!"

"I'm not afraid of the Dark Side," Ken said, as he finished getting dressed. "I'm old enough to go Topworld. I want to find out for myself what the real world is like."

"Nonsense."

While HC continued going through Ken's school files, Chip turned on the vaporizing tooth-cleaner and stuck the tip of it into Ken's mouth. "You'll be old enough to find out about the real world when Dee-Jay says you're old enough, and not a day sooner!" Chip exclaimed. "Never forget that it's the duty of us droids to take care of you and make sure no harm ever comes to you. You're a very important boy! Aren't I right, HC?"

"Indeed," HC agreed.

Ken yanked the vaporizing tooth-cleaner out of his mouth. "What makes me so important?"

"Well, for one thing, because *we* raised you," HC replied. "It isn't just *any* boy who can say he was raised by caretaker droids of the Jedi Knights. And we've allowed you to learn many Jedi secrets, I might add! Why do you think we treat you like royalty here? Like a prince—a Jedi Prince."

"Personally, I don't think *real* princes have to put up with getting tooth-cleaner pushed into their mouths every morning by some droid. And real princes have banquets, they don't just drink vitamin syrup for breakfast, lunch, and dinner."

"My, how you exaggerate," Chip said.

HC, meanwhile, continued to grade Ken's homework.

"How did I get to be with you droids anyway?" Ken asked. "And when will you tell me who my parents are?"

"Dee-Jay is the only one who is programmed to answer those questions, Master Ken. And he promised to tell you when it's time for you to know."

"But when will that be?"

"No one knows but Dee-Jay."

"And that's the way it should be," HC added, without pausing to look up.

"Dee-Jay likes to keep secrets," Ken said. "He probably won't tell me until I'm as old as Commander Luke Skywalker; or maybe not even until I'm two hundred and seven, like—"

"Chewbacca is two hundred and five," HC interrupted.

Chip put the vaporizing tooth-cleaner into Ken's mouth once again, and Ken promptly took it out.

"Did you ever stop to think that I might be tired of being cared for and protected all the time?" Ken demanded. "Especially by droids."

"I've told you a thousand times, Master Ken, I don't think," Chip said. "You certainly should know that by now."

"And I don't think, either," HC added. "I merely evaluate and process information—and give grades, of course. Fortunately, one doesn't have to be able to think in order to give grades."

Ken hopped back into his bed and positioned his pillow under his head. "Well maybe if you droids could think, it would occur to you that I'd like to have some friends who are my own age."

"Why, Master Ken, I was manufactured the same month you were born," Chip replied. "I *am* your own age."

"I meant a *human* friend. Not a robot—not a, a droid."

"Please, Master Ken. You must stop thinking about these things until it's time," Chip said. "And now is the time to wash your face, clean your ears, and drink some vitamin syrup. You've got to hurry off to the Jedi Library. Dee-Jay is waiting for you to begin your lessons."

"My ears and my face are clean. And I'm not hungry," Ken said. "And that's final. Good-bye, you two!"

Ken gave his mooka a quick scratch behind the ears. He then picked up his computer notebook and stepped out of his dome-house, *pretending* that he was heading straight for the library.

He walked along the rocky path, looking around at the huge underground cavern. Ken knew that this might be the last time he would see his home for a very long time.

As he looked around, he saw domes of all sizes, lit up by a soothing glow from bubble lights and fluorescent rocks. There were travel tubes, computer cubes, and droids of every imaginable size and shape, all going about their programmed business.

The droids were always busy—modifying the computers, making new droids, repairing old droids, working the power generators, and cleaning and maintaining the hundreds of domes throughout the city. Occasionally they even went Topworld for supplies, and to update the history of the galaxy for the Jedi Library.

When Ken reached the place where the path divided, instead of turning toward the Jedi Library, he stepped briskly toward the tubular transport shaft that went up to the surface of Yavin Four. The low-pitched whine of the shaft was almost drowned out by the loud thump of his excited heartbeat.

Ken opened his computer notebook and took out the metal key-card he had secretly made in Droid Repair Class. The key-card was the same size and shape as the one Dee-Jay always used to activate the tubular transport. Ken now had his own key-card, punched with all the correct code numbers. But would it work?

The glowing, round tubular transport was ready to make its journey straight up, through miles of Yavin Four moonrock. And Ken was ready to make the journey Topworld, to a world he had only read about in books, and seen in pictures and holograms.

He clenched his teeth and inserted his home-made key-card into the slot.

VWOOOOP!

The tubular-transport door slid open, inviting him to step inside. This was the moment Ken had been waiting for!

Suddenly he heard the clatter of metal feet approaching him from behind. "Ken, this is *very* irregular!" a familiar voice cried out.

Ken glanced over his shoulder—it was Chip!

"It's *worse* than irregular," Chip continued. "It's forbidden. You know full well you're not permitted to enter the tubular transport and go Topworld until you're a man. Besides, you didn't take your vitamin syrup. How do you expect to ever become big enough and strong enough to defend yourself?"

"But I hate the taste of vitamin syrup," Ken protested. "I want to find out what real food tastes like for once in my life. I want to have some dessert for a change. And I don't mean vitamin mints, either—I mean *real* desserts, like ordinary kids get to have. I want to see the sky, and the rain forest. I want to travel to other stars and planets."

"What would Dee-Jay say about this if he found out?" Chip interrupted in a very annoyed tone. "*I'll* tell you what he'd say. He'd say I neglected my duty and let you run off where you could be killed by Imperial stormtroopers, or eaten by wild beasts, or—"

"Chip, I'm going Topworld," Ken said insistently. "And don't try to stop me. But as long as you're here, you might as well come along. I may need a droid to help me."

DWEEP-DWEEP!

The tubular transport started beeping—a signal for all passengers to enter.

"You don't know what you'll find up there in the Topworld!" Chip said in a panic-stricken voice. "What do you know about bounty hunters, or, or—" Chip stammered, "or stormtroopers, or Imperial grand moffs, or Mynock bats, or Rancor creatures. There are alien boy-sellers who might steal a boy like you and sell you into a life of slavery in the spice mines of Kessel!"

Ken ignored Chip, and grabbed the silver droid by the arm, tugging him into the tubular transport. Suddenly the door slid shut. Ken pushed the button that said TOPWORLD, and the tubular transport began to rise like a rocket.

PHWOOOOOSH!

Higher and higher it zoomed. Ken stared out the

window. Faint lights seemed to be dancing out of the blackness, like sparks of colored fire. It was the glow of luminous rocks.

"Relax, Chip," Ken said. "This will be fun."

"Fun, Master Ken?" Chip said. "Droids aren't programmed to have fun. You should know that by now."

"Believe me, I do," Ken said in a disappointed voice.

Suddenly Ken felt as if his stomach were flying away from him. The tubular transport was going so fast it seemed almost out of control.

Ken and Chip each held tightly onto the handrails with all of their strength. "Oh, mercy," Chip said. "I was never designed to take the trip Topworld."

Ken shut his eyes and held his breath. And then, when he had held his breath as long as he possibly could, the tubular transport finally began to slow down, and then it stopped.

DZZZZZT!

The door slid open, and Ken took his first cautious steps into the rain forest.

In front of them was a beautiful wall of bright green marble. Together they went through an opening in the wall; the soft green light of the rain forest dazzled Ken's eyes.

Ken had a faint memory of having seen this rain forest before. Perhaps it was when he had been a very small child, on that fateful day that the droids had only hinted to him about, when the Jedi Master in the brown robe had carried him down to the safety of the city built by ancient Jedi Knights. There the Jedi Master had left Ken, with no reminders of his past, nothing except the crystal he wore on the silver chain around his neck. Ken didn't even have a hologram photo to remember what his mother and father looked like.

Ken continued to walk forward, leading Chip through the thickets of trees and vines, without knowing where they were going. Ken's ears welcomed the sounds of the jungle—the cawing and chirping that filled the air like a song. It wasn't long before they completely lost track of where they were and how to get back to the round stone wall of the tubular transport!

CHAPTER 3
Flying with the Force

As Trioculus's Imperial strike cruiser plunged through deep space, Grand Moff Hissa sighed with relief. It was good to be hurtling through space again. They were safe now.

Hissa's pulse quickened as he recalled the narrow escape he and Trioculus had made from the Whaladon-hunting submarine back on Calamari. They had escaped just moments before the gigantic underwater explosion caused by Luke Skywalker.

Now they were on their way to the Null Zone to see Kadann, the Supreme Prophet of the Dark Side. And three-eyed Trioculus, who had declared himself to be the new ruler of the Empire, proudly wore the glove he had found during their undersea journey—the glove of Darth Vader.

Grand Moff Dunhausen, Hissa's most-trusted commander, came hurrying over, his earrings jangling and shaking. Dunhausen always wore earrings shaped like little laserblasters.

As Dunhausen informed Hissa of a dismaying message that had just been received, Hissa bit his lip and lowered his head. Hissa would have liked to have had good news to bring to Trioculus, but it seemed good news was in short supply.

Grand Moff Hissa found Trioculus inside the ruler's private quarters aboard the strike cruiser.

"My Dark Lordship," Grand Moff Hissa began, "Grand Admiral Grunger still refuses to accept your claim to be Emperor—that is until Kadann, as Supreme Prophet of the Dark Side, officially gives you his dark blessing. In that case, Grunger will withdraw his objections and will order his fleet of Star Destroyers to follow your command."

Trioculus gritted his teeth. "And what is his excuse for withholding his loyalty?"

"Like so many of the others, my Lordship, he doubts your claim to be the son of Emperor Palpatine."

Trioculus snarled in anger. "What about COMPNOR?" he hissed in a low growl. "Has COMPNOR replied to my demand for loyalty?"

COMPNOR was the Commission for the Preservation of the New Order—a group of powerful, brutal Imperial terrorists.

"My Lordship, COMPNOR also waits to serve you until you receive the dark blessing of Kadann."

Trioculus furiously blinked all three of his eyes— his two ordinary ones, plus his third eye, which was perched in the middle of his forehead. "What more does that black-bearded dwarf want?" Trioculus stormed. "He made a prophecy that the new Emperor would wear the glove of Darth Vader, and I have found the glove—that should be enough for him!"

"Kadann may be a dwarf, but I suggest that you don't underestimate him, my Lordship," Grand Moff

Hissa offered. "Before he will give you his dark blessing, he has to examine the glove himself to make sure it's really Darth Vader's. I suggest you respect him—and be wary of him. He's crafty and sly. Expect him to try to trick you. And to test you."

With his right hand—the very hand that wore the glove of Darth Vader—Trioculus gripped a round control knob on the navigation panel.

"One other thing about Kadann, sir," Grand Moff Hissa added. "It's important that you speak the truth to him, no matter what he asks you. No one has ever deceived the Supreme Prophet of the Dark Side and lived to tell about it."

Trioculus frowned, squeezing the control knob even harder, as if he were choking a disobedient stormtrooper. The beacon at the top of his Imperial strike cruiser turned on. It sent out an intense light, sweeping across the blackness of space in search of his destination—Space Station Scardia, home of the Prophets of the Dark Side.

Luke Skywalker was just above the top of the rain forest on Yavin Four, speeding faster than his airspeeder was designed to go. Luke squinted against the onrushing wind, racing madly without giving any thought to where he was going. It was as if someone else were the real pilot of his airspeeder—as though he were being pulled by a power greater than his own.

When he looked down, the tops of the trees blended together into a streak of blurry green. The only landmarks on the horizon were the tops of the ancient pyramids.

But Luke was soon out of sight of the pyramids, lost and alone in the sky, with no understanding of where he was headed or why. Then he saw a stone sticking up very slightly above the treetops.

He slowed down his airspeeder, hovering and circling the stone.

He could see that it was like a steeple, perched at the top of a small temple hidden among the trees—a temple built by the ancient Massasi tribe of Yavin Four.

Luke piloted his airspeeder to a landing, breaking through the thick blanket of leaves at the treetops. At last he was on soft ground, near the base of the ancient temple. The floor of the rain forest was dark. The foliage was so thick the skylight couldn't shine through.

Luke felt the pull again. The Force was guiding him, drawing him to walk past the tangle of twisting vines and radiant flowers that were in front of him.

A voice inside Luke, however, told him he should go back. His conscience was telling him that Princess Leia, Han Solo, and Chewbacca would be worried about him.

But for the moment Luke followed a different voice instead. It was a quiet voice that made scarcely a sound. It was the inner voice of the Force, a voice that only a Jedi Knight could hear.

Luke left his airspeeder near the base of the temple and walked through the thick foliage.

He heard someone speak in rhyme, and he stopped cautiously in his tracks.

"You come from afar
So very welcome you are."

A strange alien humanoid with green, rubbery skin was leaning over, digging up a purple flower. When the alien stood erect, Luke could see that he was almost nine feet tall. Instead of hair, there were short, snakelike vines growing out of the top of his head.

The alien glanced at Luke and spoke again:

> *"Baji is my name*
> *I'm glad that you came."*

Luke's experience in life had taught him never to be too trusting. He put one hand on his lightsaber, unsure whether Baji was a friend, or an enemy pretending to be a friend.

"What are you doing here, Baji?" Luke asked.

> *"A Ho'Din healer am I*
> *May these plants never die*
> *From them comes health*
> *The only true wealth."*

Baji held up the purple flower just beneath Luke's nose. Luke cautiously took his hand away from his lightsaber and touched the flower. He took in its sweet, strong fragrance.

Baji explained:

> *"A Ho'Din healer never lies*
> *Kibo plants cure the eyes*
> *So rare and hard to find*
> *For the blind man, so very kind."*

Suddenly Luke noticed a silvery gleam of light shining from behind a shrub. It was something made of metal, and it was moving.

Could it be a weapon?

Luke leapt to his feet, drew out his lightsaber, and turned on its power. It was now a deadly, glowing sword, ready for battle.

"Come out from behind there, whoever you are!" Luke said.

There was the sound of crinkling leaves. Whoever was hiding in the brush was trying to crouch and keep out of sight.

"Show yourself," Luke said. "This is your last warning!"

A silver, boy-shaped droid instantly popped up from behind the bush. "This is highly irregular!" the droid exclaimed. "Do you always threaten innocent droids who are merely taking a walk in the forest?"

"Why are you spying on us?" Luke asked. "Who are you?"

"I'm not programmed to give out my name to strangers," the silver droid said.

"That's just what I'd expect a spy to say," Luke replied.

A boy who seemed to be about twelve or thirteen poked his head up alongside the droid. "Don't blame Chip," the boy said. "*I* was the one who said we should come here. But I'm warning you, if you're a soldier of the evil Empire, you'll never take me alive!"

Luke grinned. "I'm not an Imperial soldier," he said. "I've probably fought more Imperial stormtroopers than you can count. What's your name?"

"Ken," he replied.

"Ken what?"

The boy shrugged. "Just Ken. I was never given a last name by the droids."

"What droids?" Luke asked suspiciously.

"Chip, and the droids who live near my dome-house, of course," Ken said, touching the silvery crystal he wore around his neck. Then he squinted and looked Luke in the eye. "Do you always ask strangers so many questions?"

Ken brushed the leaves and thorns off his clothes and stepped out from behind the branches. Chip, whose feet were tangled in a vine, struggled to get free of the twisted plant.

"Here, let me help," Luke offered.

FWOOP!

With one quick stroke of his lightsaber, Luke cut the vine between Chip's feet, setting the droid free. Then Luke returned the lightsaber to his belt.

"Thank you," Chip said. "That's much better. But just in case you were wondering, I was about to get untangled all by myself."

"And now we'd appreciate it if you'd tell us *your* names," Ken said.

Baji spoke first:

> *"Baji is my name*
> *From the planet Moltok I came."*

"And I'm Commander Skywalker," Luke volun-

teered, "Jedi Knight and Alliance pilot, from Tatooine."

Ken's mouth fell open in shock, his sparkling blue eyes gleaming with wonder.

He dropped down on one knee and bowed his head, as if he were a serf who expected to be knighted by a great king. "Commander Luke Skywalker," he said, "I can't believe it. I thought it was you, but I said to myself no, it couldn't be. This is the greatest honor of my life!"

"You've heard of me, then?" Luke said.

"Heard of you! I've studied you! I know almost everything you've ever done!"

Luke smiled and put his hands on his hips. "Really now? I don't think even *I* remember everything

I've ever done."

"Yoda was your Jedi Master!" Ken said. "And before you met Yoda, you learned about the Force from Obi-Wan Kenobi! And you saved your sister, Princess Leia, from Darth Vader, who was really your own father, who turned to the Dark Side when—"

Now it was Luke's mouth that fell open in shock. Who *was* this boy?

"This is *highly* irregular," Chip interrupted. "Why just this morning, HC was correcting Ken's homework, and Ken seemed to know almost *nothing* about you, Commander Skywalker. He thought *you* were the pilot of the *Millennium Falcon,* instead of Han Solo. But now that he's run away from our underground home, he suddenly thinks he knows *everything* and doesn't need his droid teachers anymore."

"Why have you run away from home?" Luke asked.

"You'd run away from home, too, if your only friends were droids."

Puzzled, Luke knitted his brows and put a hand on Ken's shoulder. "The home that you ran away from, Ken—is it an underground city that was built long ago by Jedi Knights?"

But before Ken could answer, they heard a crunching noise in the forest. It was the sound of approaching footsteps.

Baji stepped back cautiously as Luke reached for his lightsaber again. Suddenly a very large and powerful-looking droid pushed aside some branches and walked toward them.

The droid's body was white, and his radiant red eyes shone like rubies. His strong, dignified metal face even had a metal beard.

"Dee-Jay!" Ken exclaimed. "What are *you* doing here?" He was so surprised, he accidently dropped his computer notebook to the ground.

"You have a great deal of explaining to do, young man!" Dee-Jay scolded. "The rules were made to protect you, to keep you safe until you are old enough."

The towering, white droid then turned to Chip. "And you, Chip," Dee-Jay continued. "You've broken my trust."

"I did my best to talk him out of coming Topworld," Chip explained timidly. "But he's a disobedient boy, with a head as hard as stone. He never takes orders, you know."

"I'd be happy to take orders from Commander Skywalker," Ken said. He glanced at the last of the Jedi Knights. "Commander Skywalker, I want to sign up with the Alliance. Will you take me with you? I want to fly in starfighters, and fight the Empire, and—"

Before Ken could say anything more, and before Luke could reply, Dee-Jay raised his hands, releasing a foggy white smoke from his fingertips.

FWISHSHSHSH!

The smoke spread instantly, creating a thick, blinding mist.

Luke coughed as he breathed the white smoke and fanned the air with his hands. Rubbing his eyes, he strained to see. But he was enveloped in the misty cloud.

Luke called out for Ken. But when the mist began

to clear, Ken, Chip, and Dee-Jay were gone.

"I've got to find Ken!" Luke exclaimed. He was convinced that Ken could show him how to find the Lost City of the Jedi that Obi-Wan Kenobi had spoken about in his dream. Luke now understood why the Force had led him to this spot.

Baji turned to Luke and spoke discouraging words:

> *"Jedi Knight*
> *Your search is in vain*
> *Gone they are*
> *Deep into the forest of rain."*

But Luke was determined to try to find out where they had gone. He began looking for a trail, for some hint of their path.

It wasn't until Luke was out of sight that Baji discovered the computer notebook that Ken had dropped on the ground. He opened it. On the inside cover, the boy had written:

This notebook belongs to Ken
Dome-house 12
South Jedi Lane

CHAPTER 4
The Dark Blessing

"Approaching the Null Zone, your Lordship," said Imperial Commodore Zuggs, the beady-eyed, bald officer who was piloting Trioculus's Imperial strike cruiser.

"Keep the cruiser's eye sensors tuned to look for Space Station Scardia," Trioculus ordered.

"Very well, sir," Commodore Zuggs replied.

Space Station Scardia was the cube-shaped distant outpost in the Null Zone where the Prophets of the Dark Side lived. At that very moment, inside the huge cube, Supreme Prophet Kadann awaited Trioculus's arrival.

Wearing his glittering, flowing prophet's robe, the black-bearded dwarf strolled slowly through one of Scardia's many corridors, on his way to the Chamber of Dark Visions. He was calmly sipping his tea, boiling tea that would have scalded the tongue of any ordinary man.

Kadann's tea was made from fungus-infested bark that came from the forest moon of Endor, where the furry Ewoks lived. Some said that it helped him dream of the future.

But Kadann's prophecies didn't always come from

dreams. The inspiration for Kadann's prophecies more often came from his secret network of very ruthless and efficient spies. They dutifully brought him secret information. This outpost was, for all intents and purposes, the Imperial Bureau of Investigation.

Information from spies helped Kadann figure out what was likely to happen. And if his prophecies didn't come true by themselves, then Kadann and the other Prophets of the Dark Side used their great influence to *make* them come true, using bribery, sabotage, and treachery—and sometimes even murder. In that way they kept their power and influence in the Empire.

When Trioculus and Grand Moff Hissa landed inside Space Station Scardia, they were met by a welcoming committee of Prophets of the Dark Side, including other dwarfs like Kadann, all the way up to High Prophet Jedgar, who was seven feet tall. The things they all seemed to have in common were their beards and gleaming black robes.

"Trioculus, Grand Moff Hissa, I trust that our worthy visitors suffered no ill effects from gamma radiation when you reached the Null Zone," High Prophet Jedgar inquired in a soothing voice. Jedgar always played the role of gracious host whenever anyone arrived at Space Station Scardia.

"There were no problems at all," Grand Moff Hissa replied. "Our ship is properly insulated from every form of radiation, including gamma rays."

The three eyes of Trioculus were greeted by the dazzling glitter of archaeological treasures gathered from all over the galaxy. Kadann's vast collection of

stolen valuables decorated every room and corridor of the space station, all arrayed in beautiful display cases.

"Is it true that Kadann has been collecting rare artifacts his entire life?" Grand Moff Hissa asked.

"Quite so," High Prophet Jedgar replied. "The baubles and trinkets in these display cases were gathered over a long span of years indeed."

High Prophet Jedgar turned and led Trioculus and Grand Moff Hissa to the Chamber of Dark Visions, where Kadann would receive them.

There they found Kadann up on a podium, seated on his ornate prophet's chair. Even with the podium, Kadann was so short he still didn't come up as high as Trioculus's chin.

At Kadann's side was a low table with many small balls resting on it. The balls seemed to be made of chalk, and each one was a different color.

"Dark Greetings, Slavelord Trioculus," Kadann said.

"Dreamer of Dark Dreams, Supreme Prophet of the Empire," Grand Moff Hissa began, "Trioculus is no longer merely the Chief Slavelord of the spice mines of Kessel. The Central Committee of Grand Moffs recognizes the mighty Trioculus as the Empire's one true leader—our new Emperor."

"And what does the mighty Trioculus want of me?" Kadann asked, though he already knew the answer.

"I've come to ask you for your dark blessing," Trioculus said. "As you once gave your dark blessing to my father, Emperor Palpatine."

Kadann picked up a yellow ball and held it in front of him. He closed his eyes and crushed the ball, which turned to powder in his hands.

Trioculus put his lips close to Grand Moff Hissa's ear. "Yellow is the color of a lie," Trioculus said. "What have I said that he doesn't believe?"

"That you are Emperor Palpatine's son," Hissa whispered. "Kadann knows the truth."

"Emperor Palpatine's son does not look like you," Kadann declared boldly.

Trioculus placed his hands carefully on his hips. "You call yourself Supreme Prophet of the Dark Side, Kadann, and yet you don't know that the Emperor fathered a son who was born with three eyes?"

"Since you ask, I shall tell you exactly what I know," Kadann said, in a forceful voice that showed not even a hint of fear. "The Emperor had a son he rejected from the day that son was born—a son he sensed might grow to become even more powerful in the Dark Side than he himself. And so he banished his son to the planet Kessel, where he was forced to work in the spice mines like a common slave." Kadann stared at Trioculus and smiled slyly. "Yes, his son was born with three eyes. In that you are correct."

Trioculus nodded with satisfaction.

"But where were those three eyes?" Kadann asked. "One was here." Kadann pointed to his own right eye with his forefinger. "And one eye was here." He slowly moved his forefinger to his left eye. Then Kadann moved his finger behind his head. "And his third eye was here, at the *back* of his head. With his third eye, he could see his enemies from behind."

Trioculus, whose three eyes were all at the front of his face, scowled.

"And you were one of those enemies, Trioculus," Kadann added. "As Chief Slavelord, you had authority over him."

Kadann picked up the red ball and crushed it in his hands. A breeze gusted through the chamber and blew the red-colored chalk onto Trioculus's clothes, staining them like blood.

"You seem to be accusing me of being a murderer," Trioculus said in a quiet but furious voice.

"Are you not?" Kadann replied in a very low voice. "Do you deny murdering Triclops, the Imperial royal son?"

Trioculus hissed beneath his breath and clenched his gloved right hand.

"Your Lordship, I beg you, remain calm," Grand Moff Hissa whispered to Trioculus. "Kadann knows many things. Whatever happens, don't become angry, or you will fail the test."

Trioculus gnashed his teeth and squeezed both of his hands into tight fists.

"The truth," whispered Grand Moff Hissa very quietly. "You *must* tell him the absolute truth. I promise, Kadann will understand."

"I may be a murderer," Trioculus said to Kadann, "but I never killed Emperor Palpatine's son."

"Are you saying that someone else killed him?" Kadann asked with a cagey smile.

"Obviously your spies haven't done their job, Kadann," Trioculus said, frowning. "They are telling you lies and misinformation. Perhaps Triclops would be better off if he were dead, but for the moment, he is still alive."

Grand Moff Hissa interrupted. "It was the secret judgment of the Central Committee of Grand Moffs that Triclops, the Emperor's son, was both mad and criminally insane. He was a menace to everyone he ever met, friend and foe alike."

"A very unfortunate situation," Kadann agreed, nodding his head.

"After Emperor Palpatine died in the explosion of the Death Star, those of us grand moffs who knew of the Emperor's wishes *had* to do something to protect what was left of the Empire," Grand Moff Hissa continued. "Did we dare let his son Triclops lead us—a son he had banished? Why if Triclops were ever put in command, I have no doubt that he would have destroyed us all—every grand moff, grand admiral . . . and every Prophet of the Dark Side! In fact, we grand moffs believe that if ever Triclops is allowed to sit on his father's throne, he'll destroy the galaxy, planet by planet, until there is nothing remaining."

The black-bearded dwarf said nothing. He sat on his prophet's chair silently, stroking his beard.

"So you see, Kadann, we were in desperate need of a new leader," Hissa went on. "We couldn't keep fighting among ourselves, warlord against warlord. The lower-ranking officers and common stormtroopers knew there were rumors that a three-eyed son existed who had a legal right to his father's throne. And so—"

"So you decided your new leader had to be a man with three eyes," Kadann said, completing Grand Moff Hissa's sentence. "Someone the grand moffs thought they could trust. One who could claim to be the Emperor's son without arousing any suspicions."

"Exactly!" Grand Moff Hissa said, breathing a sigh of relief. "That's why we asked Trioculus, Slavelord of Kessel, to claim to be Emperor Palpatine's son and to serve as our new Imperial leader. Trioculus understands full well that the Central Committee of Grand Moffs is the *real* power behind the throne."

"I have fulfilled your prophecy, Kadann," Trioculus said in a confident voice. "You foretold that the next Emperor would wear the glove of Darth Vader. And as you can see, I wear it."

Trioculus held out his right hand, thrusting the glove of Darth Vader toward Kadann.

"If you have any doubts that this is the glove of Darth Vader," Trioculus said, "then see for yourself."

Kadann touched the glove and inspected it closely. "I recognize it," he said.

"So then you are satisfied that Trioculus has fulfilled your prophecy about the next Imperial ruler?" Hissa asked.

"He has indeed. The man who wears the glove of Darth Vader shall be our Emperor." Kadann then picked up the silver ball and spoke again. "But there is another prophecy about the one who wears the glove—" Kadann stopped himself in midsentence and fell silent.

"What is it?" Trioculus insisted.

Kadann squeezed the silver ball of chalk until it crumbled to dust. "Silver is the symbol of a Jedi Prince. There is a Jedi Prince from the Lost City of the Jedi who can destroy you."

Trioculus sneered in disbelief. "The Lost City of the Jedi is only a legend!"

"A legend only to those who don't know the truth. For it does exist. And you, Emperor Trioculus, must find the Jedi Prince who lives there, or you will not rule for much longer." Kadann now raised his right hand and pointed his forefinger upward, as though uttering a commandment. "This is your destiny. Find the Jedi Prince and destroy him—or he will destroy you!"

Trioculus frowned in dismay.

"And where *is* this Lost City of the Jedi?" Grand Moff Hissa asked.

"There are four continents on the fourth moon of Yavin," Kadann replied. "The Lost City is on the largest continent, deep beneath the ground, under the rain forest. Look for a round wall made of green marble in the forest. There you will find the entrance to the city. But you must find it soon. Very soon."

"I shall," Trioculus said, putting his hands on his hips triumphantly. "Not only shall I destroy the Jedi Prince, but as ruler of the Empire, I shall rid the galaxy of Luke Skywalker and the entire Rebel Alliance."

"Well spoken, Emperor Trioculus." And with that Kadann leaned forward and kissed the glove Trioculus wore. "You have my dark blessing," he said.

Trioculus smiled. It was one of the first real smiles of his life. However, it was cut short by a stabbing pain in the center of his head. Everything then became blurry and dim. Emperor Trioculus could see only dull blobs of light, shadows, and streaks of gray— and nothing more.

CHAPTER 5
A Path of Fire

Trioculus remained still, blinking his three eyes. Within moments his vision came back to him and he could see clearly once again. Following on the heels of Grand Moff Hissa, he departed from the Chamber of Dark Visions. He acted as if nothing happened. It was a perfect act. He didn't tell anyone—not even his trusted droid, Emdee.

A short while later, as Trioculus stood in the control room of his Imperial strike cruiser and looked out at the vastness of space, his thoughts were millions of miles away. He was thinking about Yavin Four and its vast rain forests. "How can I find the Lost City of the Jedi?" he wondered aloud.

"Someone on Yavin Four *must* know where the Lost City is," Grand Moff Hissa said. "The question is, who?"

"Perhaps Luke Skywalker or SPIN knows," replied Trioculus in an icy voice.

"Yes, SPIN, of course," said Grand Moff Hissa, referring to the Senate's Planetary Intelligence Network. His eyebrows shot upward as he suddenly got an idea. "I think you should send those Rebels an ultimatum— a warning so terrible that they won't be able to ignore it."

* * *

A few days later on Yavin Four, where the next meeting of SPIN was about to take place, Princess Leia and Han Solo were already seated in the conference room, waiting for Luke Skywalker. Han was so enjoying seeing Leia again that he'd put off his return to Bespin with Chewbacca.

"Han, I'm worried about Luke," Leia said. "He promised me he was going to show up on time for the SPIN meeting today."

"I'm worried too," Han said. "Have you noticed how strange he's been acting lately?"

"Luke *has* been acting different," Leia agreed. "The way he went off on his airspeeder the other day."

"Yeah," Han agreed. "Since when does he take mysterious journeys over the jungle, without any idea of where he's going?"

"He does things like that when he feels the pull of the Force," Princess Leia replied. "And now he's obsessed with finding a boy he says is from the Lost City of the Jedi."

"I think he's gone off the deep end," Han said with concern. "Luke never used to believe in the Lost City of the Jedi. He told me that because Obi-Wan and Yoda never mentioned it, then it must be only a legend. But suddenly he's convinced that it does exist—and he thinks the Force is going to lead him to it."

At that moment, Luke hurried in to join the other SPIN members in the Senate conference room. "Sorry I'm late," he said, out of breath.

"Same excuse as usual?" Leia asked.

"Afraid so," Luke admitted. "I was on my airspeeder again, searching for Ken. Still no luck."

The SPIN meeting started with a report by Rebel Alliance leader Mon Mothma on the problem of Imperial probe droids. "There's a new danger to SPIN," she explained. "Several enemy probe droids have recently penetrated Yavin Four's Air Defense Network. They've been spotted hovering over the jungle, as if searching for something. But their purpose is still unknown."

EEEE-AAAAA-EEEEE-AAAAA . . .

An alarm siren sounded in the Senate. Security had been violated.

KCHOOOOING! KCHOOOOING!

In the SPIN conference room the sound of laser blasts could be heard coming from the big defensive laser cannons on the domed roof of the building.

BRACHOOOOM!

The laser cannons must have missed their target, because something crashed right through the roof. Luke looked up to see a very small, perfectly round, black Imperial device flying under its own power. It zoomed around the SPIN conference room like a tossed ball.

Then it hovered in front of everyone.

Han Solo raised his blaster and fired once . . . twice . . .

But the black Imperial device kept dodging his blasts with short, sudden movements, continuing to hover in midair.

From inside his Imperial strike cruiser orbiting

Yavin Four, Trioculus watched what was taking place. The floating device was transmitting the scene inside the Senate, and Trioculus could see it on a screen from inside his navigation room.

He saw every SPIN member in the conference room. Above all he saw Luke Skywalker join Han Solo, in the attempt to destroy the floating Imperial probe device.

Then Trioculus saw the face of Princess Leia.

"That face . . ." he said to Grand Moff Hissa. "That woman . . ."

"Princess Leia," the grand moff confirmed.

"A first-degree renegade and troublemaker," Trioculus said, nodding.

"Darth Vader blew up her home planet of Alderaan, so he could teach her the importance of cooperating with the Empire," Grand Moff Hissa commented. "But she never learned."

"She has a striking face," said Trioculus. "Strong features, but soft. Not at all unattractive, considering that she's a Rebel Alliance woman with only two eyes."

"She's very dangerous," Grand Moff Hissa continued. "She murdered Jabba the Hutt. *Choked* him to death with the chain that kept her prisoner."

"I never liked Jabba the Hutt," Trioculus said. "A disgusting, fat slug—and a common gangster."

The spherical device was programmed by remote control, automatically dodging the weapons that were firing at it. As Trioculus watched the screen, he saw Luke Skywalker returning his blaster to his holster and drawing his lightsaber. Skywalker, the Jedi Knight whom Trioculus had vowed to destroy, would finally die at last, in just a few moments . . . that is, unless Luke Skywalker knew where the Lost City of the Jedi could be found and was prepared to reveal the information at once. Then Trioculus would see fit to spare Skywalker's life, at least for the time being.

As Skywalker tried to strike the sphere with his blazing lightsaber, it continued to jump away. Then it projected a hologram.

The members of SPIN watched in astonishment as the image of Trioculus appeared before them.

"Attention, Luke Skywalker and members of SPIN," the image of Trioculus said, "if by any chance you deluded yourselves into thinking that I perished back on Calamari, I'm sorry to have to disappoint you. I've just sent you a little gift that has penetrated your weak security system—this Imperial Antisecurity

Device. It is armed with an explosive of awesome power. In just twenty seconds I shall detonate it and destroy the entire Rebel Alliance Senate. However, to show my good will, I hereby agree to spare your lives if one of you announces at once the location of the entrance to the Lost City of the Jedi. The twenty seconds now begins. One . . . two . . ."

By remote control, Trioculus deactivated the hologram projector inside the device. From far away in space he was still able to watch the scene inside the SPIN conference room—a scene of desperate attempts to destroy the floating black sphere.

"I doubt we'll get any information out of them," Grand Moff Hissa said. "It's obvious they're more interested in fighting than in talking."

"Commodore Zuggs, activate the heat mechanism in the Antisecurity Device," Trioculus ordered. "It will require ten seconds to reach detonation temperature."

"Heat mechanism activated, sir," Zuggs stated, wiping a thin line of sweat that was flowing from the top of his clean-shaven head.

The view on the screen turned bright red as the device began to overheat. Five seconds to zero . . . four seconds to zero . . .

At two seconds to zero Luke's Jedi powers served him well. Directing his intense concentration at the black sphere, he forced it to stop darting back and forth in midair so it was no longer a moving target. As it remained steady and still, Luke sliced it in two with his lightsaber.

KECHUNKKK!

The detonator was in shambles, unable to trigger the explosion.

Out in space, inside Trioculus's strike cruiser, the Imperial ruler scowled when he saw that his first plan for finding the Lost City of the Jedi had failed.

"Proceed to Plan Number Two," Trioculus said. "The search and destroy mission!"

The sky over the rain forest turned deep purple with the onset of twilight. However, the beautiful sky was the last thing on Trioculus's mind as he landed on Yavin Four with a large fleet of escort carriers. The escort carriers were filled with enough TNTs to carry out his Plan Number Two.

TNT was short for Treaded Neutron Torch—a treaded, tanklike vehicle that could torch the rain forest by shooting neutron fireballs. TNTs could ride right through the most intense, blazing fire, without any harm to the stormtroopers riding inside.

As soon as Trioculus gave the order, the TNTs began to go into action over a wide area.

They started to torch the rain forest on the biggest continent of Yavin Four, shooting neutron fireballs everywhere. The TNTs filled the air with fire and smoke, and began to turn the forest into a heap of ash and charred timber!

"When the rain forests have all been destroyed, we'll find the entrance to the Lost City easily," Grand Moff Hissa explained. "We'll be able to locate the round wall of green marble from the air."

With Grand Moff Hissa following close behind him, Trioculus walked down the ramp of his Imperial strike cruiser. He wanted to see the action firsthand.

Looking around, he stared at the orange glow of flames and the billowing black clouds. And then the roar of a neutron fireball almost deafened him.

He gasped and pressed the glove of Darth Vader to his face. As he rubbed his eyes his right hand inside the glove ached. But the ache of his hand was the least of his worries.

When Trioculus opened his eyes he was now totally blind. He could no longer see even a dim haze or shadowy flicker of light. This was a darkness as pitch-black as a starless region of deep space.

The droid, Emdee, examined the new Emperor's eyes in the seclusion of Trioculus's private cabin on board his spaceship. He was unable to find any sign that Trioculus's eyes had been scorched by the fire or damaged in any way. Emdee confessed that this case was beyond his medical knowledge.

"Figure out what's wrong with my eyes, Emdee," Trioculus said, gritting his teeth. "Or I will have you

taken apart and sold for scrap metal!"

"My Emperor," Grand Moff Hissa interrupted, "we have just received a report from a team of stormtroopers. Near one of the jungle pyramids they spotted an alien—a Ho'Din, to be precise. Almost all Ho'Din know how to work medical miracles using plants and herbs. They're a race of healers, your Excellency!"

"Then tell them to capture that Ho'Din," Trioculus said, pressing his gloved hand against his eyes. "He shall figure out how to restore my sight— or I shall have *him* blinded as well, so he too can share my fate!"

CHAPTER 6
A Healer's Secret

Ken risked Dee-Jay's wrath to come Topworld again. And this time he not only gave Dee-Jay the slip, he ducked away from HC and Chip, too, by convincing both droids to help him with the library research for his latest homework assignment.

The assignment was to write a report on five major planets that had been wiped out by asteroids in the last half million years. HC and Chip were still probably deep in the Jedi Library, walking up and down the aisles trying to find out where the file on destroyed planets had been misplaced, unaware that Ken had hidden it under his bed in his dome-house.

Retracing his steps from his last trip Topworld, Ken soon spied Baji in the forest. The smell of smoke was in the air. And the distant forest fire was approaching.

Ken had never seen a forest fire before, except in holograms and pictures in the Jedi Library. His heart skipped a beat as he watched in horror. So much beauty was being destroyed in the fiery orange glow.

Ken cautiously approached Baji, not wanting to be seen. But perhaps the Ho'Din healer would know where Ken had left his computer notebook. Ken was determined to find it before the droids found out that he had lost it.

"Excuse me, sir," Ken said. "I met you once before, the day Luke Skywalker was here. Do you remember me?"

Baji jumped back, taken by surprise and somewhat startled. He smiled, nodded, and then without saying a word, he hurriedly collected more plants as fast as he could.

"I didn't mean to scare you," Ken continued. "I was just wondering, did you happen to come across my computer notebook? I think I dropped it somewhere around here."

Baji put a hand on Ken's shoulder and said:

"Find it I did
In my hut it is hid
Come there with me
And your notebook you shall see."

Picking up a sack that had flowers, plant stems, roots, and seeds, Baji led Ken to his thatch hut.

The little hut was bare. Baji had only a bed of soft leaves and a simple table and chairs. However, everywhere he looked, Ken saw that the hut was piled high with bottles containing seedling plants. All the bottles and jars were labeled in a language Ken couldn't read.

Baji kneeled to pick up Ken's computer notebook. "Thanks, Baji," Ken said. "It was nice of you to save this for me. And the droid who corrects my homework, HC, will sure be happy it's not lost. HC would really give me a hard time if I told him I'd lost it."

Baji peered through the open door of his hut and looked out at the red glow of flames far away in the forest. He shook his head sadly and frowned. Then he sighed and glanced down, looking away.

Ken stared at the reddish glow shining through the thick forest. There was no doubt about it, the fire was getting closer.

"I know what you're thinking," Ken said. "If the fire reaches your hut, then all your rare plants will be destroyed."

Baji nodded.

"I wonder how the fire started," Ken said.

And the reply was:

> *"The weapons of the Empire*
> *Did cause this big fire*
> *So now the end is near*
> *For a forest so dear."*

"Come home with me," Ken said. "You'd be safer there, underground."

Baji shook his head no.

> *"My work here is done*
> *From this forest I shall run*
> *My people are on their way*
> *A spaceship comes next day."*

"I can see that you'll be sorry to leave," Ken said. "It's a shame we haven't had the time to get to know one another, but I understand. Your home is on another world."

Baji nodded and smiled.

"I've got to be going," Ken said, "before the fire gets any closer. May the Force be with you, Baji."

Ken waved good-bye and started walking back in the direction of the green marble wall, where the tubular transport would take him back to the Lost City of the Jedi right away. Ken wanted to return before HC or Chip or Dee-Jay noticed that he was gone.

Ken glanced back to wave to Baji one more time. Suddenly Ken's heart thumped wildly. Three Imperial stormtroopers were approaching Baji's hut!

What was he going to do? Ken's first impulse was to dash toward them and shout, but he knew better than that. He was sadly outnumbered. And he had no way to defend himself or Baji.

Ken ducked, concealing himself in the foliage. He saw the stormtroopers point their blasters at Baji, capture the helpless Ho'Din healer, and lead him away.

Each of Baji's two hearts was beating rapidly as the stormtroopers forced him up the ramp of Trioculus's Imperial strike cruiser. His warm green blood became hot from fear as they led him past the maze of equipment in the control room, and into the private cabin of Emperor Trioculus.

The room was so dimly lit it was hard for Baji to

see the face of the Emperor, who was seated on an ornate chair. Grand Moff Hissa smiled politely at Baji, and Emdee stared at Baji as if he were a curiosity.

"At last the Ho'Din is here," Grand Moff Hissa said to the new Emperor.

Trioculus slowly leaned forward. Baji could see the Imperial ruler's three half-opened eyes. His eyes looked glassy, and the pupils were clouded.

"Ho'Din, if you ever breathe a word of what I'm about to tell you, you'll never live to see another Yavin Four sunset," Grand Moff Hissa said. "Tell me, are you a healer, like the rest of your people?"

Baji nodded but didn't speak.

"I command you to answer!" Trioculus shouted in a hoarse voice.

Suddenly realizing that Trioculus was unable to see, Baji replied:

"For the sick and weak do I care
Be they powerful or meek, old or fair."

"They tell me you're a Ho'Din," Trioculus said, "but at the moment, I can't tell. My eyes have betrayed me. I order you to heal me!"

"This is the most powerful patient you've ever had, Ho'Din," Grand Moff Hissa explained. "He commands the Empire. He is the ruler of the galaxy. Your life is in his hands."

Baji leaned forward and stared cautiously at Trioculus's glazed eyeballs. Then he noticed the glove Trioculus was wearing on his right hand. Baji kneeled

down and touched it. Quickly Trioculus pulled his
hand away.

"I asked you to examine my eyes, Ho'Din, not
the glove of Darth Vader," Trioculus said. "Now heal
me, understand?"

Baji replied:

> *"The glove you wear*
> *Brings blindness and gloom*
> *Remove it now*
> *For it seals your doom."*

"This glove *has* doomed many men, Ho'Din,"
Trioculus said, sneering. "Men who have angered
me. But it will never doom *me*."

Baji replied:

> *"Since Darth Vader's glove*
> *You now do wear*
> *Blind you are*
> *And next goes your hair*
>
> *Take off the glove*
> *Or there is no doubt*
> *Your teeth and nails*
> *Shall all fall out*
>
> *Your hands will rot*
> *Your face will welt*
> *Loud you shall scream*
> *As in terror you melt."*

"I should have your eyes plucked out for saying that!" Trioculus exclaimed.

"Master," said Emdee, "the Ho'Din makes a medical point—one that did occur to me. The devices I inserted into the glove's fingertips so that you could send out deadly sound waves might possibly be the cause of your side effects."

"Go on, Emdee," Trioculus said, gritting his teeth, "continue."

"The sonic charges in the devices are probably causing damage to your nerve endings, affecting the optic nerves in your eyes."

"Perhaps you *should* consider taking off the glove, my Dark Lordship," Grand Moff Hissa said. "It's worth a try."

Reluctantly, Trioculus removed the glove of Darth Vader. Grand Moff Hissa and Baji couldn't help but gasp when they saw Trioculus's right hand—it was all red, blistered, and withered. And just as Baji had warned, the flesh on his hand had already begun to rot.

Trioculus blinked. The yellow, glassy look slowly faded from his eyes. "I can almost make out the shape of your face, Ho'Din," Trioculus said in a hoarse, deep voice.

"Your Excellency!" Grand Moff Hissa said. "The Ho'Din healer has brought back your eyesight!"

Baji reached into his pocket and took out a few kibo seeds—all that he had. He placed them in Trioculus's raw and withered hand. Then said:

"Eat the seeds of the purple flower
Or your sight shall lose its power
To be fully cured you must feed
For a hundred days upon the kibo seed."

Trioculus chewed and swallowed the kibo seeds. Moments later, his face brightened and his eyes cleared. A faint smile formed at the corners of his lips as his vision was slowly restored.

"Ho'Din, your medicine is impressive," Trioculus said. "I now see better than ever. Tell me, where can I get enough kibo seeds to eat them for a hundred days?"

Baji sadly lowered his head.

"Kibo flowers, so very rare
Will soon be found nowhere
For the flames that you have spread
Shall soon make all kibo plants dead."

"What is he saying, Hissa?" asked Trioculus. "I can't follow all of this Ho'Din's rhyming!"

"If I understand him correctly," the grand moff replied, "the kibo flower is very rare—nearly extinct. And your decision to burn the rain forests is about to destroy the last of them. You must eat their seeds for a hundred days, or—"

"Go on!" Trioculus said. "Then what?"

Emdee finished the sentence for the grand moff, who was too frightened to say any more. "Then, Master, you will go blind once again," Emdee said. "This time probably forever."

Once more Baji spoke:

"In my hut I have seeds in store
Enough for all your needs and more
But my hut soon shall burn
Tell me, why does the Empire never learn?"

Panicked, Trioculus ordered Baji to lead them back to his hut at once. The fire Trioculus had caused was about to destroy the last of the rare plants that were the only cure for his blindness!

Quickly they walked down the ramp of the Imperial strike cruiser and climbed aboard a mobile jungle transport vehicle. Baji gave directions. As they neared his hut, the flames were rapidly approaching, threatening to destroy the entire area.

Trioculus got out of the vehicle and hurried on foot toward Baji's hut. Suddenly one of the dozens of TNTs came roaring through the forest on its fast moving treads, firing its neutron torches.

"No, stop!" Trioculus shouted, as it aimed its front gun right at Baji's hut. "Stop, I command you!"

But the stormtroopers inside the TNT couldn't hear the Emperor. The TNT fired again, and Baji's dry, thatch hut started crackling as it burned.

A very desperate Trioculus went running into the fiery hut to save the kibo plants and seeds. But as he clutched them in his hands and tried to escape the hut, the doorway was blocked by a wall of flame.

CHAPTER 7
The Secret Code of Obi-Wan Kenobi

"If the fires in the rain forest are not contained," Princess Leia said to the members of SPIN, "then this moon of Yavin will face disaster. The rain forests are the source of our oxygen essential for the air we breathe. And thousands of medicines used throughout the galaxy are made from the rare species of plants that can only be found in these forests. There has been an invasion by a ruthless mutant—a three-eyed slavelord named Trioculus who calls himself the new Imperial Emperor. He is destroying our forests because he is on some insane mission to find the entrance to the Lost City of the Jedi. This evil madman must be stopped!"

With those words, the Rebel Alliance sprang into action. While Alliance fire fighters tried to put out the raging forest blaze, the *Millennium Falcon,* with Luke Skywalker, Han Solo, and Chewbacca aboard, searched for Trioculus's jungle base.

"I should be putting the finishing touches on my sky house right now, but instead, I'm stuck piloting the *Falcon* on another crazy mission for the Alliance,"

Han complained.

Not far behind them was a group of Alliance Y-wing starfighters. Their job: To destroy Trioculus's encampment and spaceships, giving the tyrannical dictator no hope of escape from Yavin Four.

The *Millenium Falcon* soared over the path of the spreading fire and followed it to its source. Soon Luke Skywalker located a clearing. Trioculus had taken over a Bantha grazing pasture that had been cut out of the jungle. His Imperial strike cruiser was on the ground, surrounded by a group of Imperial escort carriers. The tread marks of dozens of TNTs led away from the escort carriers in all directions.

"There's his base!" Luke said, communicating with the pilots of the Y-wings. "Go to it!"

As the Y-wings started destroying the grounded Imperial spaceships, the *Millennium Falcon* fired well-aimed laserblasts at a group of TNTs, taking them out one at a time.

The TNTs didn't just sit around waiting to be destroyed. They started firing back a barrage of neutron fireballs, blasting away at the low-flying *Millennium Falcon*. Han and Chewie had no choice but to guide the *Falcon* to an emergency landing in the forest below.

It was the worst landing of Han's career. The *Falcon* was unstable and shaking. It ripped through a maze of tall trees and thick vines, bouncing and sliding as it cut a gouge in the forest floor. "Arrrrroowgh!" Chewie moaned, knowing that the *Falcon* was now in desperate need of repair.

"Tough break, Chewie," Han agreed after the ship came to a stop. "The *Falcon's* in trouble."

Luke, Han, and Chewie made a quick exit from their spaceship. The scent of smoke was everywhere, and they could hear the explosions of neutron fireballs in the distance.

"What do you think, Han?" Luke asked. "Do you figure the *Falcon* will ever be able to make the trip again from here to the Bespin system in eighteen standard time parts?"

Suddenly Han Solo saw a gleam of white in the corner of his eye. He glanced toward the object and drew his blaster. "A stormtrooper!"

Han fired a couple of times. Chewbacca hurried

over to see what the trouble was.

Luke propped himself up so he could see. "Stop, Han! That's not a stormtrooper! It's a droid I met. His name is Dee-Jay, and he's from the Lost City of the Jedi!"

"It's a droid named what from where?" Han asked.

Dee-Jay came toward them. Ken was alongside him, carrying his computer notebook.

"Commander Skywalker," Dee-Jay said. "You see what a disobedient boy I have here. No matter how many times I tell him not to come Topworld, he keeps coming back!"

"I had to find my computer notebook," Ken said. "I didn't know there'd be a fire, and TNTs, and storm-

troopers, and—" Ken suddenly glanced at Han. He recognized him from pictures he'd seen in the Jedi Library. "Wow, you're Han Solo, right?" He then looked over at the Wookiee. "And—you're Chewbacca!"

"Groooowwfff!" Chewie said, confirming that Ken had gotten his name right.

"We know who *we* are, kid," Han said. "What we don't know is who *you* are and what you're doing here."

"I'm Ken," he replied. "And I've always wanted to meet you, Mr. Solo, for just about my entire life. You're one of the best Corellian pilots in the whole galaxy!"

"What do you mean *one of*?" Han replied. "You know anybody better?"

"Snoke Loroan made the trip from here to the Bespin system in fifteen standard time parts," Ken said, without even batting an eyelash. "The best the *Millennium Falcon* has ever done is eighteen standard time parts. I looked that up in the Jedi Library."

Han rolled his eyes in amazement. Who *was* this kid?

"Okay, okay, I'll admit I'm impressed," Han said. "But Snoke Loroan got wiped out in the battle of Endor. We're talking about *living* Corellian pilots."

"Then I guess you're the best," Ken admitted with a smile.

"You've got that right," Han said and beamed. "Now I'll tell you what, Chewie and I have flown from one end of this galaxy to the other in the *Millennium Falcon*. If you or your droid know any way we can escape from this blazing firepit, we'll give you a free ride to the planet of your choice, someday." Han thought about his offer again. "Well, almost any planet. Kessel and Hoth are off-limits."

"You've got a deal!" Ken said. "That is, if it's okay with Dee-Jay."

"Commander Skywalker," Dee-Jay said, "the flames approach. You and your friends must follow me to safety. With your help, I may be able to stop these fires."

To Luke's astonishment, without walking very far through the forest, they arrived at the circular stone wall made of green marble.

"It's just like in my dream!" Luke said. "We're at the entrance to the Lost City of the Jedi!"

"My Corellian buddies will never believe this!" Han Solo said.

Dee-Jay led them through the opening in the wall. There they saw the circular tubular transport. As Dee-Jay approached, the door slid open, and they all went inside.

"Hold on tight," Dee-Jay warned. "You may find this ride a bit disagreeable."

The tubular transport dropped so fast, Luke and his friends felt as if they'd left their stomachs behind. They plunged through an underground region in total darkness. They kept dropping at an incredible speed, and soon they saw flashes of flickering lights from luminescent rocks.

At last they came to a stop at the bottom of the shaft, several miles underground. Luke stepped out and looked

around in awe. Here it was, the place he had been searching for. And in this illuminated cavern, it still seemed as bright and new as it must have looked when the first Jedi Knights built it a long time ago.

Luke tried to take in everything at once. The many dome-houses where the Jedi Knights used to live, the platforms filled with equipment of an advanced technology, and the transport vehicles and roads made of perfectly cut stone.

Dee-Jay led them past a huge building with a sign that read: Jedi Library.

"Those of you who live on the surface of Yavin Four think the weather of this moon is the work of nature," Dee-Jay said. "But it's not. It's actually controlled from down here, from our Weather and Climate Command Center."

They entered the Climate Command building. There Dee-Jay took them down a long corridor, as droids hurried by them busily from both directions.

"Thousands of years ago," Dee-Jay continued, "Yavin Four was a cold and barren world. The Jedi Masters who built the Lost City discovered that they could change its climate. All they had to do was find a way for the heat from the core of this moon to reach the surface.

"And so," Dee-Jay explained, "they cut many deep shafts into this moon, like the shaft of the tubular transport. The other shafts are designed for releasing steam and heat into the atmosphere. Using their weather and climate control system, the Jedi Knights made this moon grow warm and tropical. They even seeded its continents, so lush rain forests would grow."

Dee-Jay now led them into a gigantic room that had a huge machine the size of a planetary power generator.

"This moon is on a cycle—a six-month dry season followed by a six-month rainy season," Dee-Jay said. "The rainy season is due to start in several weeks. But if we could discover the code to speed up the weather cycle, we could start the rainy season now."

"That would sure douse the fires in a hurry," Han commented. "And none too soon. I won't be a happy man if the *Millennium Falcon* goes up in smoke."

Dee-Jay opened a control box. "We've got to figure out the code," he said. "I've searched nearly every file in the Jedi Library, but I just can't seem to find it."

"I had a dream," Luke said. "A vision of Obi-Wan Kenobi. He told me . . ."

Luke tried to remember what Obi-Wan Kenobi had told him in his dream. *Memorize this code*, Obi-Wan had said. *Its importance shall soon become clear to you.*

But what was the code Obi-Wan had told him to memorize? Try as he might, Luke couldn't recall it.

Luke took a deep breath and then exhaled. He let all his thoughts flow out with his breath. Then, as he inhaled, he felt the power of the Force pouring into him, filling him with energy and power.

Suddenly it was there: JE-99-DI-88-FOR-00-CE.

"I remember the code!" Luke exclaimed. "Obi-Wan didn't tell me what it was for, but I sure hope it activates the weather cycle."

Luke punched in the code. And it worked!

A screen in the room lit up and showed them what was happening on the surface of Yavin Four. Steam vents opened at locations all over the Yavin moon. The vents forced warm, moist air into the atmosphere. And with astonishing speed, storm clouds began to form everywhere across the sky.

Watching the screen, they could see the rain begin to fall. Then there was lightning. A torrential storm sent sheets of water pouring down from the black clouds. Soon the rain began to put out the fires in the forest.

In the torrential rainstorm, Trioculus, Grand Moff Hissa, and Emdee made their way back to what was left of their Imperial base camp. Reluctantly Baji accompanied them. To his sorrow, with a blaster pointed at his head, he was drafted into the Imperial army to become a staff physician.

As they surveyed the scene of the destruction, Trioculus clutched his jar of kibo seeds and touched his withered right hand to his face. It was no longer the same handsome three-eyed face he'd had before.

In Trioculus's rush to get the kibo seeds from Baji's hut, his face had been horribly burned. Now his face was covered with welts and blisters, and his skin was scorched.

Trioculus recoiled in shock at seeing that his Imperial strike cruiser had been blasted apart. And every Imperial escort carrier had either been damaged or exploded.

All that is, but one. In their push to achieve victory, the Rebel Alliance had neglected to destroy a single escort carrier.

The glove of Darth Vader, which Trioculus had left in his Imperial strike cruiser, was now lying in the mud on the ground. The rain lashed at Trioculus as he knelt to pick it up.

He didn't put it back on, but he kept it.

"You're going to make me another glove, Emdee," he said. "One that looks just like the glove of Darth Vader. No one must know that I no longer wear the real glove!"

"It's regretful that we didn't find the Lost City of the Jedi, my Emperor," Grand Moff Hissa said. "But if we send enough spies to Yavin Four, they'll keep looking for it until they find it—and perhaps they'll find the Jedi Prince as well."

"SPIN must be destroyed for this attack,"

Trioculus said. "SPIN—and every member of the Rebel Alliance in their Senate! Except . . ."

"Except whom, Lord Trioculus?" Grand Moff Hissa asked reluctantly.

"We'll take Princess Leia alive," Trioculus replied firmly.

And then they climbed aboard the remaining escort carrier. Once inside, they activated the power and took off, leaving Yavin Four behind. Trioculus then laid his head back in his chair and closed his eyes.

With his face painfully burned, and his right hand crippled and withered, Trioculus escaped into a dream, a dream of the beautiful Princess Leia. He could see her striking face, her strong but soft features. And he dreamed of making her his queen—the Queen of the Empire!

The time had come for Ken to bid farewell to the Lost City of the Jedi, and to HC and Dee-Jay, the droids who had raised him with devotion. Chip was to remain with Ken, to help him when he went Topworld to join Luke Skywalker and become the youngest member of the Rebel Alliance.

Dee-Jay had always known that the day would arrive when he would have to allow Ken to leave the Lost City and go off into the galaxy to live his own life. However, he had expected to wait until Ken was at least twenty, not twelve.

But Dee-Jay understood that the time was right for Ken to depart. From now on, Luke would give Ken guidance and instruction in the ways of the Force.

It was Ken's destiny.

Zeebo jumped into Ken's arms and licked his face, just like he had every single day, for years.

"I'm going to miss all you droids," Ken said. He thought about what he'd just said, and realized that he would probably even miss HC-100 every once in a while. "And I'll miss the Jedi Library," he continued, "and my dome-house, and I'll certainly miss you, Zeebo. Life won't be the same not having a mooka to wake me up every morning. But just think— I'm off to see the galaxy. My adventures with the Alliance have just begun!"

Luke hoped Ken would always remain enthusiastic, even after he learned more about the real world. And above all, Luke hoped that Ken would remain safe from the vengeance of the Empire. They may have stopped Trioculus from finding the Lost City of the Jedi, but Luke knew the cruel Imperial ruler would never rest until he got even—with each and every one of them!

Glossary

Baji
A Ho'Din alien, a healer and medicine man who lives in the rain forest on the fourth moon of Yavin. Baji is wise, peaceful, and speaks in rhyme. He collects plants, rare stems, roots, leaves, and vines that are good for making medicines and that he fears may become extinct. He then tranports them to his home planet of Moltok, for other botanists to study.

Chip (short for Microchip)
Chip is Ken's personal droid. His outer metal is silver. He is the size of a twelve-year-old boy and is programmed to look after Ken. As much as he tries, more often than not he is unable to talk Ken out of doing adventurous things.

Commodore Zuggs
A bald, beady-eyed Imperial officer who pilots Trioculus's Imperial strike cruiser spaceship.

Dee-Jay (DJ-88)
A powerful caretaker droid and teacher in the Lost City of the Jedi. He is white, with eyes like rubies. His face is distinguished, with a metal beard. He is like a father to Ken, having raised him from the time the young Jedi was a small child.

HC-100 (Homework Correction Droid-100)
His appearance resembles See-Threepio, though he is silver in color, with blue eyes and a round mouth. HC-100

was designed by Dee-Jay for the purpose of correcting and grading Ken's homework. He walks in perfect step like a soldier on the march, and talks like a drill sergeant. He frequently pops into Ken's dome-house without any warning for surprise homework checks.

Ho'Din

Gentle, ecologically aware aliens from the planet Moltok who have snakelike tresses growing on their heads. They are primarily botanists and prefer nature to technology. Baji is a Ho'Din healer. Ho'Din natural medicine is recognized throughout the galaxy.

Jedi Library

A great library in the Lost City of the Jedi. The Jedi Library has records that date back thousands of years. Most of its records are in files in the Jedi master computer. Others are on ancient manuscripts and old, yellowed books. Gathered in this library is all the knowledge of all civilizations and the history of all planets and moons that have intelligent life-forms.

Kadann

A black-bearded dwarf, Kadann is the Supreme Prophet of the Dark Side. The Prophets of the Dark Side are a group of Imperials who, while posing as being very mystical, are actually a sort of Imperial Bureau of Investigation with its own network of spies.

Leaders of the Empire seek Kadann's dark blessing to make their rule legitimate.

Kadann made the prophecy that the next Emperor would wear the glove of Darth Vader. Kadann's prophecies are mysterious four-line, nonrhyming verses. They are carefully studied by the Rebel Alliance for clues about what the Empire might be planning.

Ken

Ken's existence has been kept a secret, and so has the location of the Lost City of the Jedi, the city in which he is growing up. His origins are mysterious and his parents are unknown to him. For some reason the droids of the Lost City have decided not to reveal this information to him until he is older. Ken has been given the impression that he may be a Jedi Prince. He doesn't know the significance of the birthstone he wears around his neck on a silver chain.

When Ken was a baby an unknown Jedi Knight in a brown robe took him to the Lost City and left him there for safekeeping. The chief caretaker droid of the Lost City, Dee-Jay was instructed to raise Ken and educate him.

Ken has certain Jedi abilities that have come to him naturally, such as the ability to cloud minds, to mind-read, and even the power to move small objects by concentrating on them.

Ken goes to school in the Jedi Library in the Lost City, where he is the only student. There he is taught by Dee-Jay. Ken is not permitted by the caretaker droids to visit the surface of Yavin Four until he is old enough to defend himself against evil.

Kibo flower

A type of very rare purple flower Baji collects. The seed from the kibo flower can restore sight to the blind.

Lost City of the Jedi

An ancient, technologically advanced city built long ago by early Jedi Knights. The city is deep underground on the fourth moon of Yavin. The entrance is marked by a seven-foot wall of green marble in the shape of a circle. Inside the circle is a tubular transport that descends to the Lost City.

All the greatest secrets of the Jedi are recorded in the Lost City, stored within the master computer of the Jedi Library. For ages, droids have been in charge of taking care of the city. The only human there is twelve-year-old Ken. However, Ken does have a pet—a mooka named Zeebo.

The existence of the Lost City has long been one of the Jedi's greatest secrets. Though Kadann knows it exists, neither he nor any other Imperial knows its location.

Moltok
The planet where the Ho'Din live. It is where Baji comes from and where he has his greenhouse.

Prophets of the Dark Side
A sort of Imperial Bureau of Investigation run by black-bearded prophets with their own network of spies. The prophets have much power within the Empire. To retain their control, they make sure their prophecies come true—even if it takes force, bribery, or murder.

Space Station Scardia
A cube-shaped space station where the Prophets of the Dark Side live.

TNTs
TNTs, or Treaded Neutron Torches, are tanklike vehicles that shoot fireballs. They were originally designed for use in the spice mines of Kessel, blasting into rock to open up new mine shafts. However, they work just as well as jungle vehicles, plowing their way through rain forests.

Topworld
An expression that refers to the surface of the fourth moon of Yavin. When the droids of the Lost City of the Jedi talk about going Topworld, they mean taking the tubular transport to the surface.

Triclops
Though Triclops doesn't appear in this book, we have learned that he is the true son of the evil Emperor Palpatine. Triclops is a three-eyed mutant, with one eye in the back of his head.

    He is shrouded in mystery. All that is known about him for certain is that the Empire considers him insane and fears disaster if he ever were to become Emperor. For some mysterious reason they still keep him alive, imprisoned in an Imperial insane asylum and a secret Imperial reprogramming institute.

    The Empire has always denied Triclops's existence, keeping him hidden away as a dark secret. But there have been so many rumors about the Emperor's three-eyed son that to put an end to the whispers and gossip, three-eyed Trioculus falsely announces he's really Emperor Palpatine's son and the new ruler of the Empire.

    The rumors, however, still persist.

Zeebo
Ken's four-eared alien pet mooka, he has both fur and feathers.

ZORBA THE HUTT'S REVENGE

PAUL DAVIDS
AND HOLLACE DAVIDS

Illustrated by Karl Kesel

The Rebel Alliance

Luke Skywalker

Princess Leia

Han Solo

Chewbacca

Ken

Chip

Lando Calrissian

Kate (KT-18)

The Empire

Trioculus

Grand Moff Hissa

Zorba the Hutt

Tibor

CB-99

Twi'lek alien

Supreme Prophet Kadann

Triclops

To Matthew, Julie, and Colin Dwyer,
and to Michael, Max, and Sam Goodman,
May your dreams always fly
  with the *Millennium Falcon . . .*

CHAPTER 1
The Droidfest of Tatooine

Luke Skywalker's Y-wing starfighter zoomed through deep space, on its way to Cloud City for Han Solo's housewarming party.

Han's sky house was finally built. It was now floating in the air two miles away from Cloud City, on the planet Bespin.

"I've got it!" Luke Skywalker exclaimed, as he adjusted their flight path. "I know what we can get Han as a housewarming gift. We'll get him an ultra-high-density household communication screen!"

The twelve-year-old Jedi Prince strapped into the seat alongside Luke shook his head no. "Sorry, Commander Skywalker," said Ken, "but Han already has two of them."

"Oh. Well, scratch that idea then," Luke said, disappointedly. "In fact, scratch all ten of the ideas I've come up with so far."

Ken closed his eyes, forcing himself to concentrate. What about getting Han a holo-projector? Or a deluxe power booster for one of his two cloud racing cars? Or what about a supercharged multidirectional laser blaster?

Suddenly Ken bolted upright, pulling against his straps. "I know what we should get Han!" he declared. "A housekeeping droid!"

"A housekeeping droid!" the golden droid, See-Threepio echoed. "Now there's a *brilliant* idea!"

"Droids make very practical gifts," added Microchip, Ken's silver droid whom Ken had called Chip for as long as either of them could remember.

"*Tzzzooop bcheeeech!*" tooted Artoo-Detoo, the barrel-shaped utility droid, signaling his agreement.

The vote from the three droids aboard the spaceship was unanimous: All in favor, none opposed.

"Well, I don't know," Luke said, knitting his eyebrows. "Han has been a bachelor all his life. Do you think he'd want a droid around to live with him?"

"What does being a bachelor have to do with it?"

Ken asked. "A housekeeping droid isn't like having a wife. It's just a robot."

"*Just* a robot?" Chip piped up, offended. "After all we droids have done for you, Ken, you call us *just* robots?"

"The fact of the matter is," replied Threepio, "Han Solo knows *nothing* about keeping a huge house clean. He'll need help desperately. He can't expect Chewbacca to be cleaning up after him all the time! Why, Han and Chewie can't even keep the cockpit of the *Millennium Falcon* straightened out! If you ask me, a housekeeping droid is the perfect solution."

"Okay, you've convinced me," Luke replied. "But now comes the hard part—choosing the droid."

Luke activated the star map on their navigation screen. "Artoo, cool the hyperdrive thruster power," Luke said. "We're going to glide straight into Mos Eisley Spaceport on Tatooine."

"Why do you want to land on Tatooine?" Ken asked, confused. "Aren't there droid discount stores near Han over in Cloud City?"

"I guess you've never heard of the Droidfest of Tatooine," Luke said. "That's the place to go. It's loaded with JDTs."

"What does JDT mean?" the boy inquired.

"Jawa Droid Traders," Luke explained. "The droidfest is the jawas' annual sale. They have the biggest selection of droids in the galaxy. And the best prices."

"Come to think of it, I read something about the

droidfest once," Ken said, nodding. "There was a file on it in the master computer, back in the Jedi Library."

Ken had learned many things from the files of the Jedi Library, practical things, such as how to repair a droid that has a glitch in its speech mechanism. And unusual things, such as why mynock bats that live on asteroids sometimes fly upside down.

And he'd also discovered some carefully guarded secrets—secrets of the Imperial High Command, secrets that even Trioculus, the evil three-eyed tyrant who now ruled the galactic Empire, would never want anyone else to know.

Dee-Jay, the droid who was Ken's teacher in the Lost City, had warned Ken not to reveal those secrets to *anyone*—including Commander Luke Skywalker, who was Ken's guardian now that Ken had departed from the Lost City and joined the Rebel Alliance.

It wasn't long before they landed on Tatooine, the planet with the twin suns where Luke had grown up.

They docked at Mos Eisley Spaceport, at a Y-wing landing bay. Then Luke, Ken, and the droids made their way through the crowd, bumping into aliens of all shapes and sizes in the corridors of the busy terminal.

At the landspeeder rental booth, Luke got them a vehicle that was large enough for their entire group—and with an empty seat in the back for the housekeeping droid.

As Luke steered above the burning sands, they

rode along swiftly on a cushion of air. In the distance Ken could see what looked like tall metal buildings.

"Those are sandcrawlers," Luke explained. "They're jawa vehicles with tank treads. They're parked for the droidfest, very close to the palace where Jabba the Hutt used to live."

"Who lives in Jabba's palace now?" Ken inquired.

"It's vacant," Luke said, "except for the Ranats that scurry around chewing on the furniture and drapes. You see, when Jabba died, they never found his will. So the government of Tatooine took possession of his palace. For awhile they turned it into the Tatooine Retirement Home for Aged Aliens. But there wasn't enough money in the budget to keep it open."

"Didn't Jabba the Hutt also own the Holiday Towers Hotel and Casino in Cloud City?" Ken asked, remembering something he had read in the Jedi Library.

"For a kid your age, you sure know your history," Luke said. "Jabba *did* own that casino. But when Jabba died, Holiday Towers was taken over by the government of Cloud City. My old friend, Lando Calrissian, runs it now. He's the governor of Cloud City."

The sandy plain near the vacant palace of Jabba the Hutt seemed to have as many droids as there were stars in the galaxy.

The JDTs had set up colorful tents in front of their huge sandcrawlers, showing off their droids and displaying their merchandise. Luke, Ken, and the three droids went from one tent to the next. The tents rippled in the breeze, like hundreds of waving flags.

They examined HSDs, Housekeeping Specialist Droids, of every size and description. They looked at male droids, female droids, old units, even brand new ones with every possible modern capability.

But one droid seemed to stand out above all the others—a female droid named KT-18. She didn't seem to be made of metal; her body was the color of a pearl. She was clearly a top-of-the-line HSD.

"Actually, nobody calls me KT-18," the female droid said in a nice voice. "I go by the name Kate."

"Kate," said Luke. "I like that. We're thinking of purchasing you to serve a good friend of ours," Luke explained. "He's a professional pilot. Have you ever met any Corellian cargo pilots before?"

"Dozens of them," Kate replied. "My first master repaired Corellian spaceships, and I met *all* the pilots who came into his shop. Before they met me, most of them were rude bachelors with no manners. But I straightened them out."

"Really?" Luke said, surprised.

"One of them even got married because of me. The last I heard, he had six children!"

"Well, Kate," Luke said, "if I buy you as a gift for Han Solo, you'd better lay low when it comes to giving him advice about manners and marriage and stuff like that. If you overdo it, he'll probably shut down your power unit and advertise you for resale."

See-Threepio got permission from the regional

manager of the Jawa Droid Traders to open up Kate's back panel and check the quality of her circuitry.

"Excellent microcircuits," Threepio declared. "Superb mobility, too. It's rare to find a female droid who's been manufactured with such quality and—"

"Now, Threepio," Luke interrupted. "I've read the manufacturing statistics. There's absolutely no difference between the quality of materials used to make male and female droids. I'm sorry if that's a blow to your pride."

"That's quite all right, Master Luke," said Threepio. "We droids have no pride. Only a sense of honor and duty."

The jawas knew Kate was worth a lot, and they drove a hard bargain for her.

Just as Luke finished making the deal, a cloud of swirling sand appeared from behind the old, empty palace of Jabba the Hutt.

But it wasn't a desert storm. The sand was being kicked up by the hooves of dozens of lumbering four-legged Banthas. The Banthas were beasts of burden, huge elephantlike creatures with big tusks. And on their backs were tall Tusken Raiders hollering war slogans and charging to attack with waving spears!

The regional manager of the JDTs began babbling frantically in the jawan language. "It's a land dispute," Threepio translated. "The sand people say this is their holy burial ground. But the jawas say this land used to belong to Jabba the Hutt, and so it now belongs to the government. They claim it's perfectly legal for them to hold their droidfest here."

Legal or not, the Tusken Raiders seemed determined to put a stop to the droidfest. Their Banthas trampled the jawas' tents. They kicked and stomped, knocked over droids, and speared several jawas. And then they went after Luke and Ken.

"Watch out, Ken!" Chip shouted.

Ken dodged a jawa spear, and it just barely missed him.

"Now you can see why none of us wanted you to leave the Lost City!" Chip cried frantically.

"Ken, get all our droids into a sandcrawler!" Luke shouted.

Ken quickly led their four panic-stricken droids, including Kate, into the shelter of a big, treaded vehicle.

Meanwhile, Luke fought on, outnumbered and surrounded.

CHAPTER 2
The Return of Zorba

Zorba the Hutt imagined the life of luxury that awaited him in his son Jabba's mighty palace.

It would be a life of rich, greasy foods, cooked in vats of Bantha fat and served in Jabba's banquet hall. There would be slaves to bathe him every month, relaxing in the pure, cool water that Jabba stole from the moisture farmers of Tatooine.

Zorba's old spaceship, the *Zorba Express*, approached the security sector near Jabba's palace on Tatooine. He activated his communicator, about to make contact with the palace and identify himself.

"Attention, Jabba, come in. It's your papa, Zorbá. Do you read me? Over!"

But there was no reply. In the old days, Zorba thought, whenever he had requested permission to land, there had *always* been an immediate reply from Jabba.

What could this silence mean?

Zorba landed not far from the main entrance. He turned off the power in his craft, but the bell-shaped Huttian spaceship kept rumbling and clattering. *CHIZOOOOOK! SQUEEEEGE!* The ancient spaceship wheezed like a sigh from the chest of a dying Hutt.

Zorba squirmed out of the spaceship hatch. Then he began his slow crawl to the huge, thick front door of the palace.

When Zorba announced himself at the palace door, a mechanical eyeball popped out through a small opening.

"Please state the nature of your business," the mechanical eyeball said in a very businesslike tone.

"My business, as you call it, is that I am Jabba the Hutt's father, and I've come to see my son!"

"I'm sorry, Jabba the Hutt no longer lives here."

Zorba snorted. Obviously this mechanical eyeball was broken and in need of repair. Everybody knew that Jabba would never move from his palace.

"What do you mean Jabba no longer lives here?!" Zorba stormed.

"The palace is under new management," the mechanical eyeball replied. Then it moved here and there, studying Zorba from several directions. "Are you a Hutt?" it asked. "Indeed, you seem to be a Hutt!"

"Well, of course I'm a Hutt!!" Zorba shouted, his eyes bulging in anger. "How could Jabba's father be anything but a Hutt?"

"That's what I thought you said," the eyeball replied. "I'm sorry. No Hutts are allowed here anymore! New policy. No exceptions. Good day, sir!"

At that, the eyeball retreated and a metal cover slid into position to hide it.

Zorba pounded on the door. No Hutts allowed? Zorba had never heard of such an outrage!

Zorba knew that Hutts were disliked. Imperial officers often snickered whenever they talked about the planet Varl, the pockmarked planet where most Hutts lived. They said no alien creature of good breeding had ever been born on Varl. Once Zorba even heard an Imperial grand moff say that he considered Hutts to be immoral, nasty, domineering, and power hungry.

Zorba shuddered when he heard insults like that, because he considered them lies. Hutts were a proud sluglike species—very generous to their fellow Hutts, even if they were stingy and cruel to everyone else. And above all, they expected everyone—even mechanical eyeballs—to treat them with respect.

Zorba had to get to the bottom of this at once. He boarded the *Zorba Express,* and flew directly to Mos Eisley Spaceport, figuring that would be the best place to get information on the whereabouts of his son, Jabba.

Arriving at Mos Eisley, Zorba wobbled up to the big round doorway of the crowded cantina. Thanks to Jabba the Hutt, the new door was now big enough for Hutts. Jabba had threatened to shoot down one arriving spaceship each week unless the cantina door was enlarged so that he could fit inside. His request had gotten quick attention from the spaceport authorities.

As Zorba entered he noticed an Imperial grand moff standing by the bar of the cantina, talking to a group of alien bounty hunters. The grand moff was bald, with sharp, pointy teeth. He was pointing to a poster that said: WANTED BY EMPEROR TRIOCULUS! A JEDI PRINCE NAMED KEN FROM THE LOST CITY OF THE JEDI! GENEROUS REWARD!

"Grand Moff Hissa," said a Twi'lek alien, who had a long tentacle growing out of his head. "Do you know what this Prince Ken looks like? Or how old he is? Where does he come from? Did he get his name from Kenobi? Perhaps he is a relative of Obi-Wan?"

"I'm sorry, I'm not authorized to release that information," Grand Moff Hissa replied, seeming to cover up for the fact that he didn't know. "However, I *am* authorized to reveal that the Empire believes that Ken may have departed from the fourth moon of

Yavin with Luke Skywalker. The two of them are almost certainly traveling together!"

"AHEMMMM!"

Zorba cleared his throat. All eyes turned to look at his huge, wrinkled body, with its braided white hair and white beard. They stared at his enormous reptilian eyes, and his lipless mouth that spread from one side of his face to the other.

"I am Zorba the Hutt, father of Jabba! I want someone to tell me where I can find my son!"

An awkward hush settled over the noisy cantina.

"I was told that Hutts are no longer permitted in Jabba's palace!" Zorba exclaimed. "Who owns the palace, if not Jabba?"

A green-skinned bounty hunter named Tibor, a Barabel alien who was wearing a coat of armor over his reptilian skin, took a big gulp of his drink. "If I were you, Zorba," he said, "I'd calm down. Have yourself a drink of zoochberry juice."

"I will *not* calm down!" Zorba screamed. "I want information about Jabba! And I'll pay five gemstones to anyone who talks!"

The offer suddenly turned everyone in the cantina into an authority on Jabba. Dozens of voices began blurting out all sorts of things at once.

But there was one voice that stood out above all the others. "You seem to be about the only creature this side of the Dune Sea who doesn't know that Jabba the Hutt is dead," Grand Moff Hissa said.

Zorba clutched his chest. "Dead?" Was his heart

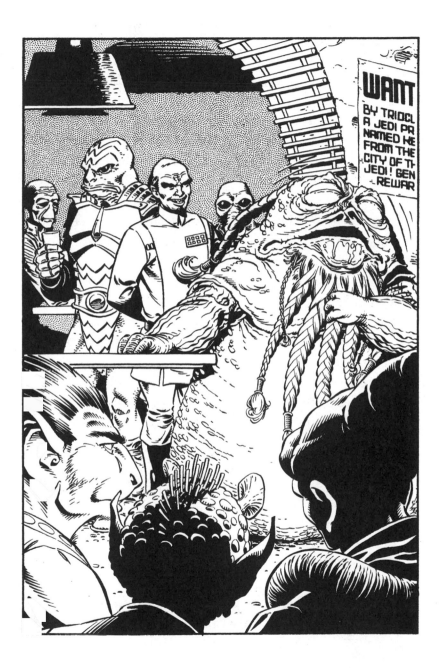

going to explode? "My son . . . *dead*?"

Zorba let out a wheezing sigh of grief that vibrated the whole room. "How did Jabba die?" he demanded.

"He was murdered by Princess Leia," a Jenet said, scratching the white fuzz that covered his body.

"Yes, it was Leia!" an Aqualish alien agreed.

"She killed him in cold blood!" Tibor shouted, pounding his body armor with a green fist.

"Princess Leia was Jabba's slave," the Twi'lek alien explained. "She had a chain attached to her. And she took the chain like this . . ." The Twi'lek twisted his own tentacle about his neck, to demonstrate. "And she squeezed the breath out of Jabba. It happened in his sail barge at the Great Pit of Carkoon."

Zorba's yellow eyes bulged from their sockets. "In the name of the ancient conqueror, Kossak the Hutt, I swear that this Princess Leia shall die!"

The bounty hunters murmured and exchanged approving glances. Then Zorba stared at Grand Moff Hissa. "Tell me, Grand Moff. Who is living in my son's palace?"

"Unfortunately, Jabba didn't leave a will," Grand Moff Hissa explained, "so naturally the Planetary Government of Tatooine took custody of his property—with the permission of the Empire, of course. At the moment, the palace is in ruins. Only the Ranats live there now."

"Ranats!" Zorba spit on the cantina floor in disgust. "I want ten bounty hunters!" Zorba announced.

"Ten strong men or aliens to come with me to Jabba's palace! I will pay seven gemstones each!"

There were more than ten volunteers. And each of them wanted to be paid before setting foot outside the cantina.

Zorba refused their request. "If any man or alien among you doesn't trust me to pay up once the job is done," Zorba threatened, "then I don't need you!"

The volunteers decided to take their chances. But all the way from the cantina to Jabba the Hutt's vacant palace, they argued among themselves about whether they had acted wisely. Most of them thought that they should have at least demanded a deposit of a few gemstones.

After a hot ride across the scalding desert in an old sail barge, they arrived at Jabba's palace.

Tibor aimed his portable anti-orbital ion cannon at the thick front door.

KABAAAMMMMM!!

The cannon blasted a hole in the door—a hole big enough for Zorba to squirm through.

Inside the palace, dozens of hairy Ranats scurried for safety at the sound of the explosion. They hid in the dark stairwells and palace closets, clutching their long rodent tails in terror.

The bounty hunters followed Zorba into the dry and dusty palace, which was in ruins. The Ranats had chewed the splendid Corellian carpets, clawed the expensive wall hangings from Bespin, and torn apart the custom furnishings from Alderaan so they could eat the stuffing.

In the palace banquet hall, it was too dark for the bounty hunters to see. And there was no longer any power in the ion surcharge generators.

But Zorba could see. His son had the walls of the palace built with ultraviolet luminous stones. Even though ultraviolet light is invisible to humans and most alien species, Hutts *are* able to see by ultraviolet light.

And so Zorba made his way to the far end of the banquet hall. There he opened a secret door, and then crawled into a hidden room.

With a gloating smile, Zorba reached out to touch a dusty old barrel-shaped droid that had been there since before Jabba was murdered.

He flipped a switch behind the droid's domed head.

TZZZZZZT!

With the power turned on, the droid was reactivated.

"Zizeeeeep!" the droid tooted.

"Tell me, CB-99," said Zorba. "Do you still have all of your memory banks? Including file JTHW?"

"Zizoooop!" the droid beeped.

"Excellent. The fools! They shall learn that Jabba's will was here in his palace all along—right inside of you!"

Zorba gave a belly laugh—a laugh so deep and loud, one might have thought he was watching a prisoner being dropped into a vat of carbonite.

"A-HAW-HAW-HAWWWW! . . ."

CHAPTER 3
Han Solo's Housewarming Party

For hours Luke Skywalker and Ken had been listening to the *KA-CHANGGGGGING* sound of the treads of a hot, grinding sandcrawler.

The Tusken Raiders, whose weapons are quite primitive, were unable to force their way into the jawas' huge, cumbersome vehicle. When Luke had found himself outnumbered by the attacking sand people, he had taken the wise defensive action of leaping into the sandcrawler and slamming shut the thick, metal door. Ken and the droids, already safe inside, were relieved to see him.

Inside, the sandcrawler was hotter than a nanowave oven. Tatooine's twin suns nearly cooked Luke, Ken, and the droids.

"All I can say, Master Luke," Threepio commented in a whiny voice, "is that if you hadn't taken refuge in here with us, I'm afraid I'd be put up for sale to a new master come tomorrow morning."

This particular sandcrawler was one of a fleet of jawa sandcrawlers heading back to Mos Eisley Spaceport the long, slow way. But under the circumstances, it was the most practical way for Luke, Ken, Threepio,

Artoo, Chip, and Kate to escape and return to Luke's Y-wing starfighter, so they could still reach the planet Bespin in time for Han Solo's housewarming party.

By the time they reached Mos Eisley, it was nighttime. In fact, it was so late that the cantina was closed.

There wasn't even anyone on duty at the land-speeder rental desk. Luke left a note explaining that, due to a sudden attack by Tusken Raiders, he was forced to leave the landspeeder at the droidfest. He hoped the Tatooine Planetary Insurance Company would cover expenses for getting it back to Mos Eisley. If not, they could bill him on Yavin Four, care of SPIN—the Senate Planetary Intelligence Network.

But just as Luke, Ken, and the droids were approaching the docking bay where Luke's Y-wing was parked, two bounty hunters jumped out from the shadows with blasters drawn.

The bounty hunters, one of them a Twi'lek alien and the other an Aqualish, sprayed the area with laserfire. Instantly Luke drew his lightsaber and extended its blazing blade.

"Well, well, Luke Skywalker," said the Twi'lek, "just as expected." He wagged his tentacle with anticipation. "Trioculus has offered a reward for Ken, the Jedi Prince. He said he'd be with you!"

Luke leapt and did a somersault in midair, landing right between the two bounty hunters.

They never knew what hit them.

Luke swirled in a circle so fast that he was only

a blur in the corner of their eyes. His lightsaber struck them both in one swing.

CRASSSSSHH! The bounty hunters hit the ground at the same moment.

"Come on, let's go!" Luke said to Ken and the droids. "Before any of their friends get the same idea!"

Luke opened the hatch, and they all popped into the Y-wing, with Artoo-Detoo next to him in the copilot position. "Set course for Bespin, Artoo," Luke shouted.

"*Bzoook!*" Artoo beeped.

A moment later Luke activated the main thrusters. Their spaceship quickly departed from Tatooine.

When Tatooine seemed to be just a small glowing ball in outer space, floating between two fiery suns, Luke put the spaceship into hyperdrive. Then they quickly accelerated past the speed of light.

Luke glanced over at Ken. "Do you have any idea why Trioculus is after you?" he asked.

Ken shook his head no.

"That three-eyed dictator practically burned down all the rain forests on Yavin Four trying to find you," Luke went on. "Somehow he found out that you're traveling with me. He's even got every bounty hunter in the galaxy on your tail." Luke glanced at Ken's downcast face. "You must have *some* idea why he believes you to be such a threat to him."

Ken shook his head no again.

"But you do know, Ken," said Chip. "It's quite irregular for you to hide the truth from an officer of the Rebel Alliance. Especially a commander, like Luke

Skywalker, who's accepted the job of protecting you. Very irregular indeed."

Ken swallowed hard. "I'm a threat to Trioculus because I know too much about him."

"Such as?" Luke asked.

"Things I learned in the files of the Jedi Library—back in the Lost City," Ken answered mysteriously. "My droid teacher, Dee-Jay, told me I was not to tell anyone, Commander Skywalker— not even you."

"Not even me?" Luke said in a hurt voice. "What is there that you can't share with me, your guardian and protector? I take my responsibility to you very seriously."

"I'm sorry, Commander Skywalker," Ken replied. "But if I told you certain things, it would make your life even more dangerous than it already is."

Luke nodded, then clamped a hand on Ken's shoulder. "I understand, Ken," he said, though he didn't really understand. But he hoped that, in time, Ken would open up more and decide not to keep any secrets from him.

The planet Bespin was located just off the Corellian Trade Route. After Luke downshifted from hyperdrive, he pointed out Bespin's two largest moons, H'gaard and Drudonna. They were known as The Twins.

Bespin was aglow in a rainbow of color. Luke explained that it was a type of planet known as a gas giant, with a liquid metal core. The metal was rethin, and the core was called the Rethin Sea. The Rethin Sea was warm—not boiling hot, like the deep interior of most planets.

Most of Bespin was gas, or atmosphere. And Cloud City had been built to float in the sky of Bespin. It was held afloat by powerful repulsorlift generators.

The city was built in levels. At the top were the hotels, spas, clubs, shops, museums, and casinos. That's where the tourists and wealthy visiting gamblers stayed.

The lowest levels were called Port Town—a dangerous place, home of Cloud City's underworld; those levels were filled with bars and industrial loading docks. There were also casinos for sleazy gamblers and outcasts down on their luck.

As soon as Luke's Y-wing landed in Cloud City, they were met by Governor Lando Calrissian.

"Well, look who just dropped in from hyperspace," said Lando, his hands on his hips as he beamed a broad smile. "The Jedi Knight from Tatooine. And you've got company with you, Luke. Who's the short guy?"

"I'm tall for my age," Ken piped up. "They call me Ken."

"And they call me Baron Administrator Calrissian, Governor of Cloud City. But if you're a friend of Luke's, you can skip the formalities and call me Lando."

"Pleased to meet you, Lando," Ken said, reaching out to shake his hand.

As they spoke, Ken was distracted by a silvery

gleam from a hazy, distant cloud. It looked like a building floating in the sky.

"That wouldn't be Han's sky house by any chance, would it?" Ken asked, pointing toward what he saw.

"It would indeed," Lando said, grinning. "That faint, black speck in that swirling cloud over there is where Han camps out these days—Han Solo's personal stomping grounds in the sky."

Ken squinted and tried to pick out more details, but he could scarcely see the house, the air was so brown with haze.

"We call it *braze*," Lando explained, as if reading Ken's thoughts. "Short for brown haze. It's air pollution. And it's becoming a serious problem here in Cloud City."

Luke, Ken, and the four droids followed Lando, walking along a ramp toward Cloud City's fleet of

cloud car convertibles.

"Highly irregular to have brown air on a planet such as this," Chip commented.

"I certainly agree," Threepio added. "It's fortunate we droids aren't organic creatures. At least we don't have to *breathe* this discolored, chemical-ridden atmosphere."

"What causes the braze, Lando?" Ken asked.

"If you're looking for somebody to blame it on, blame Trioculus—the power-mad tyrant who's now running the Empire. Trioculus has stepped up war production on a huge factory barge floating on the liquid core of this planet."

"You mean on the Rethin Sea?" Ken asked.

"Bright kid," Lando said, shooting a glance at Luke. Then Lando looked back at Ken. "The Rethin Sea is full of rare metals and Tibanna gas," Lando continued, "and Trioculus is mining them to make Imperial war machines in his factories down below. He gets his mass-produced ion cannons, and we get stuck with the smelly braze." Lando sighed. "I sent him two messages asking him politely to please shut down and go away. But Trioculus doesn't understand the word 'polite.' He told me if I ask him again, he'll invade Cloud City and take us over."

Lando opened the door of a green cloud car convertible. "Well, friends, I'm loaning you an official government car for you to fly over to Han's party. Climb aboard."

"Aren't you going to the party with us, Lando?"

Luke asked.

"Later. Tell Han I'll be by in a few hours." Lando pointed toward a tall building—the Holiday Towers Hotel and Casino. "I've got some police business to check on. A greasy little Rodian alien has a new system for cheating at the card game of sabacc, and he's trying to break the bank at Holiday Towers again."

At Han's private cloud the spectacular housewarming party was already in full swing. A true intergalactic affair, there was dancing, music, friendly conversation, and plenty of zoochberry juice.

The floating sky mansion was filled with humans, aliens, and droids, all bumping into one another's elbows, claws, fins, flippers, and metal arms.

In the center, the most comfortable chair ever designed—a sort of gigantic floating pillow—was reserved for the guest of honor, Princess Leia. Her eyes were closed for the moment, letting the gentle rocking motion relax her and help her for a few moments to forget her worries about SPIN's plans and secret projects.

Beneath Leia's floating chair, Han was playing the role of a busy host, making sure that everyone's zoochberry glasses were full, and catching up with his buddies from his home planet, most of whom were bachelor Corellian cargo pilots. One by one he introduced everyone to Princess Leia.

Meanwhile, Admiral Ackbar, the sad-eyed Calamarian fishman, stood in front of the band and talked on and on about the military strategy that helped win the Battle of Endor for the Rebel Alliance.

But nobody was paying much attention to Admiral Ackbar—especially when Han began to open his housewarming gifts.

Every few minutes Han had to jump up and run to the kitchen to check on the gourmet feast he was cooking on his nanowave stove.

Then Chewbacca put on a chef's apron and took over the cooking, so Han could dance with Princess Leia.

The band knew all of Han's favorite Corellian folk dances. Han even taught Leia how to do the Space Pirate Boogie.

When they were both out of breath and laughing from dancing so hard, Han asked the band to play "Sweet Lady from Alderaan." He thought it would make Leia happy, because Alderaan was her home planet. But instead it brought tears to her eyes as she remembered how the Empire had used the Death Star to blow the entire planet of Alderaan to pieces.

Then Leia started coughing. "Are you all right, Princess?" Han asked, worriedly.

"It's the braze," she said. "The air pollution on Bespin seems to be getting worse."

"Chewie," Han shouted, poking his head into the kitchen. "Turn up the power on the repulsorlifts. Take the house up another hundred feet or so. The air will be cleaner up there . . ."

"Grooowwwrrr!" Chewie agreed, reaching for the repulsorlift controls over by the wide window that looked out on the brown sky.

"Han, you can't spend the rest of your life here going up higher and higher in the sky, trying to get away from the braze," Leia said. "That's just running away from the problem."

"Well, that's the code we Corellians live by," Han said with a laugh. "If you can't do anything about the problem, run!"

"It's not funny, Han," she replied. "What will you do when you get up so high that the air is too thin to breathe?"

Han shrugged. "I guess I'll worry about that day when it comes. And until then—how about another dance, Princess?"

And that's when Luke Skywalker and Ken showed up with the droids—Threepio, Artoo, Chip, and Kate.

When the hugs and hellos were over, Luke introduced Han to his housewarming gift. Han was overwhelmed. He asked Kate to demonstrate some of her modern housecleaning techniques. "Of course, Master Han," said Kate. "Do you see that stain way up in that corner of the ceiling?"

Han squinted and noticed the mark.

Kate fired a vaporizing beam from her fingertip. The stain instantly disintegrated. "A small sample of my many skills," said Kate. "But I'm best at washing dishes, cleaning windows, and restoring stained carpets."

"Incredible," Han said, proudly putting his hands on his hips.

Kate seemed to think just as highly of Han.

"You're the most handsome Corellian cargo pilot I've ever met," Kate said.

"Now don't get jealous, Leia," Han said with a mischievous grin. "Looks like you'll have to get used to the fact that I'll be living with another woman from now on."

"As long as she's a droid with metallic microcircuits, I think I can keep my jealousy under control," Leia replied, with an equally mischievous grin.

As everyone got swept up in the excitement of the party again, Admiral Ackbar tried to snare Ken. He thought Ken would be a good audience for his war stories of how the Rebel Alliance blew up the Empire's Death Stars. But Ken tricked Threepio and Artoo-Detoo into keeping Ackbar company, while he and Chip ducked away to tour the house with Princess Leia.

"We can't even see the skyline of Cloud City with all this braze in the air," Ken said in a disappointed tone.

Then Leia noticed a new pair of long-range macrobinoculars that someone had given Han as a gift. They enabled a person to see details several miles away. She handed them to Ken. "Try these," she said.

Ken raised the macrobinoculars to his eyes and looked out the window. Suddenly, in spite of the braze, the view was incredibly clear. Ken could now see all the details of the distant skyline. Then he spotted a bell-shaped space vehicle approaching Cloud City.

"Hmmmmm. That's really unusual, Princess Leia.

I think I see a Huttian spaceship," Ken said.

"How do you know it's a Huttian spaceship?" Chip asked, as Luke came over beside them.

"Because I've studied spaceship designs back home," Ken said, lowering the macrobinoculars so he could see Luke. "It's shaped like a bell with a big door. It's large enough for a big, fat Hutt to get in or out."

"That's very strange," said Leia. "The Hutts almost never come to Cloud City anymore."

"Why not?" Ken asked.

"They used to come here all the time," Luke explained. "That was when Jabba the Hutt was alive and owned the Holiday Towers Hotel and Casino. But ever since Jabba died and Cloud City took over Holiday Towers, all the free-spending Hutt gamblers stopped coming here. They felt they weren't very welcome anymore."

"Here, take a look," Ken offered.

"Thanks," Luke said, taking the macrobinoculars.

Luke flipped a small button on the side of the macrobinoculars. Now they were powerful enough for him to read even the name on the side of the spaceship: *Zorba Express.*

CHAPTER 4
A Friendly Game of Sabacc

The *Zorba Express* wobbled as it settled onto a landing bay in Cloud City.

CHIZOOOOOK! SQUEEEEEEEEEGE!

As the ancient, bell-shaped space voyager let out a long wheezing sound, the Cloud City Space Dock attendants exchanged an amazed look.

For an express spaceship, it certainly wouldn't be able to take many more express journeys. In fact, after a few more trips, it was doubtful it would even be able to break the sound barrier anymore.

From out of the hatch of the *Zorba Express* came a very odd trio. First came Zorba the Hutt, who at once began coughing, because of the braze.

Then came CB-99, the slightly bent, barrel-shaped droid following Zorba. He rolled along while Zorba squirmed his way across the wide platform.

Last came Tibor, the bounty hunter, his shiny armor strapped tightly around his horny green scales.

Their destination: The Holiday Towers Hotel and Casino.

Soon they entered the lobby, which was filled with noisy, glowing games of chance. This was where the rich gambled: slickly dressed aliens in colorful costumes, wealthy business beasts from the moons of Mima, and snobby humans who brought their droids along to pull the handles of the jingling Spin-and-Win machines.

Zorba attracted quite a few stares as he wobbled up to the main desk, licking the drool from his chin with his thick dark tongue. He began a conversation with a fancy clerk droid.

The clerk droid's body glittered with polished gems. Nothing but the best for the Holiday Towers Hotel and Casino. "May I help you, um, sir?" the clerk droid asked.

"I want the passkey to Jabba the Hutt's suite!" Zorba demanded. "It's the penthouse suite."

"I'm sorry, but the penthouse suite is no longer reserved for Jabba the Hutt," the clerk droid replied. "And I am not at liberty to give anyone the passkey."

Zorba scowled. "I won't put up with rude remarks from droids! You're speaking to Zorba the Hutt, Jabba's father! And Holiday Towers is now my property!"

"Perhaps you're not aware of the change of ownership of this establishment," the clerk droid responded. "The government of Cloud City took over this hotel and casino after Jabba the Hutt died." The droid's metal face gave a programmed metallic smile. "Governor Lando Calrissian runs Holiday Towers now. And he lives in the penthouse suite. I'm sorry, but I can't oblige you."

Zorba spit on the polished marble floor. "Notify that thief, Lando Calrissian, that Zorba the Hutt is waiting to talk to him! He'll find me at the sabacc tables!"

A short while later, Lando arrived at the game room in the lobby. As he approached the sabacc tables, he saw the huge Hutt with the braided white hair and white beard. And right alongside Zorba the Hutt were Tibor and the dusty, barrel-shaped droid, CB-99.

Zorba was playing sabacc, and he was losing. Lando watched Zorba open his pouch and take out some gemstones to buy more credits for gambling.

"Hello, I'm Governor Calrissian," Lando said,

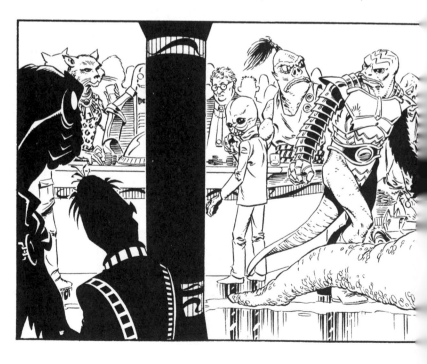

introducing himself.

Zorba's drooling tongue slid across his mouth as he hissed: "I'm Zorba, Jabba the Hutt's father. Get your things out of Jabba's penthouse suite now, because I'm moving in. And tell the clerk droid at the front desk to give me a passkey, or my friend Tibor here will send what's left of you to the nearest Cloud City mortuary."

Lando knew that there was no way to reason with a Hutt. The only way to get the better of a Hutt was to trick him, outsmart him, or wound his pride.

Lando had been around Cloud City casinos long enough to know how to recognize a miserable sabacc player when he saw one. And from the number of

gemstones he had seen Zorba lose, it was obvious that Zorba was an amateur, totally inexperienced at the game.

If Lando could talk Zorba into settling their dispute by playing a game of sabacc, then getting rid of this meddlesome Hutt would be a breeze.

"Tell you what, Zorba," Lando offered. "I'm a gambling man and a fair sport. I challenge you to a game of sabacc. If you lose, you agree to get out of the casino, leave Cloud City, and never come back."

"And if *you* lose the game," Zorba said to Lando, "*you* will leave Cloud City and never come back. And before you go, you'll appoint me as your replacement as governor! Do we have a bargain?"

Lando scratched his chin, thinking it over, recalling the time he'd gambled away the *Millennium Falcon* to Han Solo in a sabacc game. But Lando had learned a lot about sabacc since then. In fact, he was now the best player in Cloud City, second to none.

"We have a deal," Lando said with a grin.

Zorba spit into the palm of his right hand and held it out toward Lando. "Shake on it, then."

Lando's heart sank as he thought about having to touch Zorba's saliva-covered hand. He held up two fingers like a Junior Galaxy Scout. "What if I just say, 'Cross my heart and hope to die'?" Lando asked.

"Then you will die."

Reluctantly Lando spit into his own palm. And in the most disgusting moment of his life, Lando clasped Zorba's scale-covered hand and shook it.

Then Zorba opened up his pouch that had the gemstones and took out his own deck of sabacc cards.

"What's that deck for?" Lando asked.

"We play with *my* deck," Zorba replied.

"Now wait just a minute," Lando protested. "We're in the Holiday Towers Hotel and Casino. So we'll play with a deck that belongs to the house—"

Zorba wagged his fat tongue and chuckled. "I *own* the house," he said. "This is *my* casino, therefore we shall use *my* deck."

"You don't have any legal claim to this casino," Lando replied. "Jabba the Hutt died without a will. This hotel and casino automatically belongs to the government of Cloud City."

Zorba roared out a belly laugh.

"A-HAW-HAW-HAWWW! . . ."

Then, with his huge, glaring reptilian eyes, Zorba glanced at the barrel-shaped droid at his side. "CB-99, show Lando the hologram of your file called JTHW— *Jabba the Hutt's Will!*"

As instructed, the little droid projected a hologram into midair.

It showed the bloated, wrinkled face of Jabba the Hutt, reading his will. His instructions for what to do with his property upon his death were perfectly clear: *"Since I have no wife or children,"* the hologram of Jabba explained, *"if I should die before my dear father, then everything I own shall belong to Zorba the Hutt, including my palace on Tatooine, my hacienda in Mos Eisley City, the Holiday Towers Hotel and Casino in Cloud City, and—"*

The list of Jabba's possessions went on and on.

Then the hologram ended. And with it Lando's self-confident mood also ended.

Zorba laughed again, exposing the inside of his slimy mouth. "A-HAW-HAW-HAWWWW! . . ." he roared. "Just as I said, since *I* own the house, we shall play with *my* deck of sabacc cards!"

Lando's heart sank again. He inspected Zorba's deck—twice. And to his surprise, he couldn't find anything wrong with Zorba's sabacc cards.

Was it possible that it wasn't a rigged deck after all, Lando wondered?

Lando wasn't able to discover the answer. He did discover, however, that it was the worst day he had ever lived. He lost every single round of the game. His foolish bet had wrecked his life.

Lando didn't know—or even suspect—that Zorba had won because the deck had marks that could only be detected by a creature that could see ultraviolet light!

For the moment, all Lando knew was that within an hour of his losing, he was up in his penthouse suite for the last time, packing his things, ready to depart forever. And now Governor Zorba the Hutt was running the hotel and casino—and all of Cloud City!

CHAPTER 5
Trioculus's Factory Barge

Han Solo was disappointed that his party ended without Lando Calrissian ever showing up. But he was delighted with his housewarming gift, Kate, the housekeeping droid.

The guests departed, except for Han and Chewbacca's closest friends. And within two hours, the evidence of Kate's hard work could be seen in every room.

The floors were suction-cleaned, the dishes were sanitized, the trash was compacted and recycled, the leftover food was preserved in a cooling chamber, and thank-you messages were written for each and every single one of the presents Han had received.

"Roww-groooowwf!" Chewbacca howled, with a big smile.

"You're right, Chewie," said Han Solo, shaking his head in amazement. "No way that I could make it as a homeowner without the help of a housekeeping droid like Kate!" Han gave Luke a nudge. "Thanks a lot, old buddy. You sure had a good idea!"

"Don't thank *me* for the idea," Luke said. "Thank Ken. He thought of it."

"The idea just popped into my head," Ken explained, smiling. Both Luke and Han gave Ken an appreciative pat on the back.

"I hope you will all give credit where credit is due," piped up the golden droid, See-Threepio, in a jealous tone, turning to face Han. "*I* was the one who finally persuaded Luke of the merits of Ken's idea. I pointed out that you and Chewbacca seldom keep the cockpit of the *Millennium Falcon* neat and tidy. Without a housekeeping droid, in two weeks your house would end up looking like the trash compactor on board the Death Star. Do you remember when you were trapped in the trash compactor, and I said—"

"Yes, yes, I remember, I remember—" Han said quickly, shutting Threepio up. "My thanks to you, too, Threepio."

"*Bzeeepooosh!*" beeped Artoo-Detoo.

"And to you, too, Artoo," Han added. Then he put his arm around Princess Leia. "And Princess, thank you so much for coming. The party wouldn't have been the same without you."

"I wouldn't have missed it for anything," she replied. Leia smiled and gave Han a peck on the lips.

Han smiled back and gave her a long kiss in return.

BZZZZZZZZZZZZ!

Han's communication beeper was buzzing. Oh no, he thought. Who could be calling me now?

"Excuse me, folks," Han said. "I'll just be a minute."

Han went into his bedroom, where an ultrahigh-density household communication screen was located. He tuned in the large wall screen, and received the incoming message.

An image of Lando's face popped onto the screen, and he didn't look very happy.

"Sorry I missed your party, Han," Lando said. "But a whirlwind of trouble came along and set my head spinning."

"What's wrong, Lando?" asked Han.

"This is good-bye, old buddy. My political career in Cloud City has just come to an end!"

"What are you talking about? You can't just leave! You're Cloud City's governor!"

"I only wish that were true," said Lando. "I blew it, buddy. Remember how cocksure and self-confident I was the day I bet the *Millennium Falcon* and lost it to you in a sabacc game? Well, I had another attack of extreme self-confidence today—and I bet my position as governor in a game with Zorba the Hutt, Jabba the Hutt's old man."

Han's mouth fell open. "Jabba the Hutt's father? That old slug? Nobody's seen him for years!"

"Well, he's back. And the bad news is, he aced me. So Zorba is your new governor. Cloud City is sure to go to ruin." Lando glanced at his watch. "I'm on my way. My bags are packed, and my spaceship for the Zabian System is all set to leave."

"But what'll you do, Lando? You're out of a job!"

"Don't worry about me," Lando replied. "I've

still got a few tricks up my sleeve. I've been thinking about trying my hand at the theme park business."

A shocked expression swept over Lando's face. He could no longer put off telling Han the worst news of all. "Han, I overheard Zorba talking. He found out that Princess Leia killed Jabba. He's got the look of revenge in his big, ugly reptilian eyeballs. Whatever you do, don't let him find out that Leia is here on the planet, or she's a goner, for sure!"

CLICK!! The screen went black. It was the end of the message.

All the color was drained from Han's face. He called Luke and Leia into the bedroom and told them the news in private.

"We'd better get you off this planet, Leia—and fast!" Han said. "With Zorba out for revenge, he won't be satisfied until he succeeds. And if he manages to get his big ugly Hutt hands on you, it's your funeral!"

Suddenly, on the other side of the door, they heard Ken scream out, "Oh no! Kate!" Then Ken came bursting into the bedroom without even knocking. "Commander Skywalker!" Ken yelled frantically. "Kate fell!"

"What? Fell? How?" Luke asked.

"She was outside cleaning the observation balcony," Ken explained. "And she leaned over and fell into the clouds!"

"I'm going after her!" Luke shouted.

Luke hurried out the front door and walked along the yard platform. Struggling to keep his balance, he headed for the cloud car convertible he had borrowed from Lando, taking Han's macrobinoculars with him.

Luke leapt into the car. Then someone jumped into the seat alongside him. "Leia. But I thought you'd stay behind and—"

"Move it, Luke. Or she'll be halfway down to the Rethin Sea."

Luke powered up. *WHOOOOOSH!*

The cloud car took off and plunged down into the clouds at a steep angle, straight into the thick braze.

Luke triggered the hyperaccelerator. Now they were zooming faster than a droid would fall.

Luke aimed the cloud car pointing straight down, and accelerated even more.

Soon, through the misty braze, they could see Kate falling down below.

Once Luke had been saved from a fall at the bottom of Cloud City. He had tumbled right into the hatch of the *Millennium Falcon* as it flew underneath to rescue him.

Now he used the same strategy to rescue Kate. He flew the cloud car convertible beneath her, adjusted his angle and speed, and ever so gently she plopped right into the back seat.

"How can I ever thank you?" Kate asked, calmly. "But what will Master Han Solo say? I fell down on the job."

"You sure did," Princess Leia said. She pointed straight down, as the cloud car convertible kept descending. "You fell practically all the way down to the Rethin Sea. Look down below—there's the liquid metal core of the planet."

"And look over there!" Luke said excitedly. "There's Trioculus's factory barge!"

The barge was vast—a huge metal platform floating above the Rethin Sea. And on the platform were several dozen enormous factories.

The barge was an Imperial base for making weapons and ammunition—antivehicle laser cannons, Comar tritracker artillery, anti-orbital ion cannons, field missile launchers, and turbolaser emplacements. All molded from rethin and other metals found in Bespin's liquid core.

Towering above the factory barge were smokestacks, thick and tall, spewing out foul clouds of brown gas.

"Now that we're here, let's take a closer look," Princess Leia suggested.

"How about some other time?" Luke said.

"We're this close, Luke. We might as well see if we can come up with any ideas on how to stop this braze."

Luke reluctantly agreed. It was a bold idea on Leia's part. Maybe too bold, Luke thought.

As they flew nearer, their cloud car was observed down below. Suddenly the laser defense system of the factory barge came to life.

Luke swerved to dodge the blasts, but he was much better at piloting spaceships and landspeeders than cloud cars. They were hit.

The underside of their vehicle was cracked down the middle. For the moment Luke still had control, but they were losing altitude fast.

Steering frantically, Luke made their car weave in and out among the smokestacks. The car took another hit from laserfire, and within seconds, it smashed into the barge.

SCREEEEEECH! came the sounds of metal scraping metal.

The cloud car convertible skidded along a road on the factory barge. At last it came to a crashing halt, right in front of a factory covered with brown soot.

"Don't look now," Luke said, "but we've got

KARL KESEL

company coming up the road."

It was a vehicle full of Imperial stormtroopers policing the area, looking for the cloud car they'd just shot down.

In a flash, Luke, Leia, and Kate were out of the car, hurrying along the road on foot.

And just as fast the stormtroopers reached the wrecked cloud car, swarming all around it. Then they divided up to hunt for the passengers who'd escaped.

At the same moment, Luke suddenly spied their best hope for safety—a narrow tunnel with a ladder that went straight down, a sort of passageway underneath the factory barge.

Kate popped down the tunnel first, to make sure the ladder was safe. Then Leia started to descend.

Luke sensed danger close behind him. Without hesitating, he drew his lightsaber, raising the bright green laser-sword threateningly. Three stormtroopers were fast approaching.

As Luke fought with two of the Imperials, the third strormtrooper reached into the tunnel and pulled Leia back up. From down below in the darkness, Kate could see Leia dangling and gritting her teeth, as the princess kicked and swung her arms.

Leia's feet reached the safety of the metal floor of the factory barge, but her enemy had her in his grip. No sooner had Luke toppled one of their foes with his lightsaber, than he felt another one of the stormtroopers shoving him, pushing him right down into the tunnel.

Luke plunged, reaching out with one hand to

grab the rungs of the ladder.

"Oh no, Commander Skywalker," Kate screamed, "you're going to—"

But before he toppled into Kate, Luke broke his fall, just in time to see the stormtrooper slam a metal cover over the top of the tunnel, leaving them in total darkness.

CHOOOIIIIIING!

A clamp twisted over the tunnel cover. Outside, on the surface of the factory barge, the stormtrooper who held Leia then turned a valve.

"Luke!" Leia screamed, her voice muffled by the metal.

TCCHHHHHHHHHH . . . Poisonous gas flowed from the factory, through the valve, down a pipe, and directly into the tunnel.

In the darkness, Luke climbed the ladder and pounded on the cover that sealed him in. But it was closed tight. There was no way out.

"You're an organic creature, you have to breathe!" Kate exclaimed. "But if you breathe the poison, you'll die!"

Luke held his breath, closed his eyes, and concentrated. He focused his thoughts on the Force.

Luke knew how to move objects using the Force. He had learned how to do it in Yoda's swamp back on the planet Dagobah, while training to be a Jedi Knight. Perhaps now he could use the power of the Force to move the latch that held the tunnel cover in place.

As Luke desperately held his breath, nothing

happened, at first. But then the Force was with him. The clamp holding the cover shut began slowly to slide loose.

Clinging to the ladder, Luke pushed up on the cover. Then he leapt out and gasped for air. Kate climbed up the ladder to follow him out.

Together they looked around in all directions, trying to find the princess. But the stormtroopers had taken Princess Leia away!

CHAPTER 6
A Tale of Two Captives

While Han was waiting for Luke and Leia to return with Kate, he showed Ken his two streamlined cloud racing cars in his cloud car garage. One was blue, the other red.

"If I enter the Cloud Car Racing Finals," Han explained, "I'll probably drive my blue car—the Custom Model-Q Foley." Han opened the door on the driver's side of the blue car. "Want to see what it feels like to sit at the controls?"

"Thanks, thanks a lot!" Ken said. And as he settled into the comfortable, cushioned seat, he asked Han, "How old do you have to be to get a license to drive a cloud car?"

"Eighteen for humans," replied Han. "Twenty if you're an alien. Except for Biths. They let Biths drive at age ten because they're advanced bipedal craniopoids who reach maturity at a young age."

"In that case, I wish I were a Bith," Ken said. "Say, what does this do?" He touched a green button near the steering mechanism.

FWEEEEP!

"That's the—whoops, too late," Han said.

The garage door opened. Through the braze Ken could see the distant skyline of Cloud City. The city seemed to be calling out to him, urging him to seek adventure.

Han leaned into the car to check the clock on the dashboard. "I'm getting worried about Luke and Princess Leia," he said. "They've been gone a couple of hours already. It shouldn't have taken them *this* long to rescue Kate and come back."

"Maybe they decided to stop off in Cloud City for a bite to eat," Ken suggested, putting his hands on the sleek, shiny steering mechanism.

"I certainly doubt it," said Han. "There was a ton of food at my party, and plenty of leftovers."

"But Princess Leia hardly touched a bite of your Corellian cooking," Ken said.

"Why was that?" Han asked, somewhat hurt.

"She says Corellian food is too fattening," Ken explained.

"Oh, yeah?" Han said, glancing down to see if he was getting a pot belly. "You don't see any fat on *me!*"

Suddenly Chewbacca poked his head through the door to the garage. "Rowwwwrf! Groouuuuf!" he moaned.

"You're kidding!" Han said to his Wookiee friend, then glanced back at Ken. "Luke sent us a distress call. They're in some kind of trouble. My beeper was turned off, so we didn't get the message until Chewie here checked the machine just now."

Han put a hand on Ken's shoulder and said,

"Wait here, kid. I'll be back in a flash."

But Han didn't come back in a flash.

So Ken decided to pretend he was driving the cloud racing car he was sitting in. He gripped the controls. He leaned forward. And he put his hand on the acceleration lever, touching it ever so lightly.

But the light touch was all it took to power up the car and send it zooming out of the garage, into the open sky, and off toward Cloud City.

In the Jedi Library, Ken had spent many hours reading about how to fly cloud racing cars. Now he was able to make a couple of wide loops, spinning rolls, and upside-down maneuvers, all for real.

Before he knew it, he was almost all the way to Cloud City. And he almost collided in midair with a cloud bus.

OOOOO-EEEEE! . . . OOOOO-EEEEE! . . .

A Cloud Police siren blared loudly.

The police car aimed an invisible tractor beam at the cloud racing car Ken was driving.

Ken was towed to a landing bay at Cloud City. "You sure don't look eighteen, kid," one of the Cloud Police said. "Do you have the registration for this vehicle?"

"This was all just a mistake, officers," Ken said.

Ken explained that he had come to Bespin with Luke Skywalker. And that he had been driving Han Solo's cloud car totally by accident.

"Trioculus offered a big reward for a Jedi Prince named Ken who's been traveling with Luke Skywalker,"

one of the Cloud Police said to the other. "There're Wanted posters for this kid on at least a dozen planets."

And so they arrested Ken for reckless driving without a license. His destination: Cloud City Police Headquarters.

Back at Han's sky house, Han was frantic.

"Threepio, take my red cloud racing car—the Model-X1 Zhurst," Han ordered. "Bring Artoo and Chip with you, and go find Ken. He's probably taken off for Cloud City. Chewie and I will take a ride in the *Millennium Falcon* to find out what happened to Luke, Leia, and Kate!"

On the factory barge, Princess Leia was inside Trioculus's private chamber, high up in the tallest of his factories. The room had modern Imperial art and elegant furniture.

The three-eyed tyrant, Trioculus, gave a sly smile as he stared at his lovely captive.

"Please be seated, Princess Leia," he said, trying to make his gruff voice sound pleasant. "I hope you'll find these quarters comfortable."

Leia refused his invitation to sit. Instead she stared out the window, trying to avoid looking at him.

"What's happened to Luke?" she asked nervously.

"A most unfortunate situation," Trioculus replied soothingly. "We made every effort to save his life, but alas, it was to no avail."

"Do you expect me to believe that Luke is dead?" she said angrily, turning to look at Trioculus's three eyes.

"Sadly, your Luke Skywalker has departed from the world of the living," Trioculus explained. "But if it's any consolation, he died a quick and painless death."

"I don't believe a word you're saying," Leia snapped. "I would know it if Luke were dead. I would feel it."

"Perhaps not. Down here, by the Rethin Sea, feelings are dulled. All feelings—that is except my feelings for *you*, Princess Leia!"

"You don't *have* any feelings," she said. "You're a murderer! A liar! An inhuman monster!"

In a fit of fury, Leia slapped his face. Trioculus just stood there, watching her without stirring.

Leia cringed as she looked at the Imperial ruler. She had seen holograms of him in intelligence briefings, and when Trioculus sent a personal warning to the SPIN conference room in the Rebel Alliance Senate. The holograms had depicted Trioculus as devious but handsome. Handsome, except for the strange, mutant third eye in the middle of his forehead. But now his face was scarred.

She looked away, unable to bear the sight of him. However, Trioculus couldn't take his three eyes off her. He found Leia's strong but soft features to be beautiful.

Trioculus was convinced that in time he might be

able to bridge the gap between their opposite worlds. If she stayed with him long enough, eventually she might renounce the Rebel Alliance. And perhaps then she would even come to accept the necessity of evil. Especially if he were to marry her and make her the Queen of the Galactic Empire!

Trioculus took a few steps toward her. "Is it so wrong to be a murderer?" he asked. "Or a liar? Or an inhuman monster? I may be all of those things, but I still have a heart."

"Your heart is as dark as carbonite!" she hissed.

Trioculus glanced at his right hand, which now wore a replica of the glove of Darth Vader. He wondered if he should put that gloved hand on her shoulder, to show his affection for her.

"There can still be great beauty in a dark heart," Trioculus said, reaching out with the glove and gently touching her. The princess pulled away at once. "I'm certain there's darkness in you, Leia," he continued. "You're a murderer also. You killed Jabba the Hutt in cold blood, assassinated him with hatred in your heart. See yourself for what you really are!"

"I killed that thug Jabba in self-defense," she protested. "He was the most corrupt and vile gangster in the universe!"

"There's always an excuse the first time one murders," Trioculus said. "But the first murder is never the last. Why, I think you'd even like to murder me, right now. That's what you're thinking, isn't it, Leia?"

Trioculus put his hand on her shoulder once again. But she took it down right away. Then he squeezed her hand and didn't let go.

"I love you, Leia," he said in a fiery voice. "I want you to marry me and become the Queen of the Empire!"

Leia shuddered. "You're insane!" she replied.

"Accept me, Leia," he said. "I'm the only one who can give you the power and happiness you deserve!"

Leia pulled her hand away with disgust.

"You'll change your mind, Princess," Trioculus stated, refusing to lose hope that she would eventually accept his offer to be the Empire's dark queen. "There's still time for us," he said. "A great deal of time!"

CHAPTER 7
The Battle for Princess Leia

Zorba frowned as he stared out the window of his penthouse suite and slurped his sour brew. The braze outside was almost as thick as his drink, and the braze of Cloud City was the reason he had to drink the foul potion for his sinuses in the first place.

Something had to be done to persuade Trioculus to shut down his factory barge, or interplanetary tourists would find other planets that had casinos where they could spend their credits—planets that didn't have air pollution like the braze of Bespin.

Zorba had finished half his brew by the time Tibor came to see him. "I've just come from Port Town, Zorba," Tibor said excitedly. "I've learned some valuable information from an Imperial spy. Information that's worth at least five gemstones."

"Two gemstones," Zorba said. He reached into his pouch and tossed two valuable stones at Tibor's feet, as though they were no more important than glass marbles.

"Thank you, Zorba," Tibor said. "The murderess who killed Jabba the Hutt was taken captive by

Trioculus! At this very moment, Princess Leia is a prisoner on the Imperial factory barge!"

Zorba sputtered and spit out a mouthful of brew. This *was* exciting news.

"If only I had something Trioculus wanted badly," Zorba mused. "Something I could trade for the princess."

"I have an idea that's worth at least three more gemstones," Tibor offered.

"One more gemstone," Zorba corrected, as he reached into his pouch once again and tossed yet another stone onto the floor.

"Thank you, Zorba," Tibor said. "Here's my idea. I found out a little while ago that your Cloud Police arrested a boy who's been traveling with Luke Skywalker—a boy named Ken. Does that call something to mind, Zorba?"

"The Wanted poster in the Mos Eisley Cantina on Tatooine!" Zorba exclaimed. "Grand Moff Hissa said Trioculus would pay a generous reward for Ken!"

"Exactly, Zorba," said Tibor, "and what if the reward you demand is Princess Leia!"

Zorba laughed with delight. "A-HAW-HAW-HAW! . . ." But then Zorba stopped to think. "But what if this boy named Ken isn't the Jedi Prince Trioculus wants?"

To settle that matter, Ken would have to be questioned. And so Tibor took a message from Zorba to Cloud Police Headquarters, demanding that the boy be surrendered to Tibor so he could bring Ken to Zorba's penthouse suite.

Upon his arrival Ken was defiant. He threw back his shoulders, crossed his arms, and looked away from Zorba and Tibor.

But old Hutts like Zorba knew a lot about human child psychology. Zorba began the questioning by trying to make Ken feel at home.

"Such a shame a boy like you got into trouble," Zorba began. "Perhaps we can straighten it out. AHEMMM! My throat is so dry. I think I need a glass of imported Bantha milk. Bantha milk and cookies! How does that sound to you, Tibor?" he asked, winking at the bounty hunter.

"Sounds delicious," Tibor said, playing along.

"Does it sound delicious to you, too, Ken?" Zorba asked.

Ken considered his situation. Several hours had passed since Han's party. And he *was* getting hungry.

"Do you have any candy-flavored buns?" Ken asked. "I've always wanted to try them—or sticky sweetmallow?"

"Such a tasty idea! I was just going to suggest that!" Zorba lied.

He mumbled something to Tibor, whispering in the bounty hunter's ear. Then Tibor notified the Holiday Towers room service droids to bring up a tray of Bantha milk, sticky sweetmallow, and candy-flavored buns baked with avabush spice—a powerful truth serum!

When the snack arrived, Ken quickly gobbled down three candy-flavored buns!

Zorba talked on and on about how the braze of Bespin was having a bad effect on the tourist trade. And then, when Zorba felt he had waited long enough for the avabush spice to put Ken in a truthful and cooperative mood, he began by asking some serious questions.

"Tell me, my boy," Zorba said. "Are you a Jedi Prince?"

Ken brushed his moppy brown hair out of his eyes and said, "I don't know for sure, sir. I don't know who my parents were. The droids never told me."

"Which droids?" Zorba asked, rolling his big yellow eyes suspiciously.

"The droids who raised me."

"Raised you? Where?"

"In the Lost City of the . . . I mean, well, it was somewhere on Yavin Four. Or Yavin Three, I mean."

Zorba gave a devious smile. "Tell old Zorba the truth now. Hutts can get very nasty when boys lie."

"Yavin Four. I grew up in the Lost City of the Jedi," Ken continued, yawning as though he had suddenly become sleepy. "It's deep underground, in the middle of the rain forest. When I was little, I think my parents were killed in the Great War, but no one ever told me who they were. I think maybe my name, Ken, comes from *Ken*obi. I might be related to Obi-Wan Kenobi, but I don't know because the droids who raised me wouldn't tell me. All they told me was that a Jedi Knight in a brown robe took me to the Lost City for safety, so the Imperial stormtroopers wouldn't find me and . . ." Ken yawned again. "Do we have to talk about this anymore?" he asked. "I'm feeling so tired."

"You've told me enough," Zorba said. "There's no doubt about it. You're Ken, the Jedi Prince I've heard so much about." Zorba laughed with delight. "A-HAW-HAW-HAW! . . . Put him in one of the cells in the basement, where we keep the casino crooks we catch!" Zorba instructed.

"Of course, Zorba," Tibor replied.

"And then contact Trioculus on the factory barge. Tell him we have Ken, the Jedi Prince. Tell him if he still wants the boy, he should come to Cloud City so we can negotiate a deal!"

Zorba tossed one more gemstone at Tibor's feet.

"Thank you, Zorba!" Tibor said.

* * *

When Trioculus got the news, he locked Princess Leia alone in his factory barge chamber, leaving fine food and beverages for her. Then he departed for Cloud City at once, taking twenty stormtroopers with him as bodyguards.

Later that same afternoon, Trioculus and his bodyguards entered the Holiday Towers Hotel and Casino. The stormtroopers waited in the hall outside Zorba's penthouse suite, while Trioculus and Zorba bargained for their prisoners.

"I hear you are the new governor of Cloud City," Trioculus began. "Congratulations. I'm sure you will bring discipline and prosperity to the gambling industry here."

"And congratulations to you, Trioculus," said Zorba, "on becoming the new leader of the Galactic Empire."

The formalities out of the way, Trioculus then told Zorba he had come to make a deal for Ken. But first he wanted to meet Zorba's prisoner, to make certain he was actually the Jedi Prince.

Zorba instructed Tibor to take Trioculus to visit Ken in the cell in the Holiday Towers basement.

"A boy?" Trioculus said in surprise, as he first set his three eyes on the prisoner. "Why, you hardly look more than twelve or thirteen."

Ken pouted, refusing to reply.

Trioculus frowned. He had thought the Jedi Prince would be a man. How could this boy possibly be any great threat to his reign? But Kadann, the Supreme Prophet of the Dark Side, had warned Trioculus that he must quickly find the Jedi Prince named Ken and destroy him, or the Jedi Prince would destroy Trioculus! That was the prophecy. That was Trioculus's destiny!

"Don't be afraid of me," Trioculus said with a cunning smile. "I've come to Cloud City to help you. But first you must answer some questions."

Ken crossed his arms defiantly.

Trioculus heard static in his mind, static sent by Ken to attempt to cloud his thinking. And then Trioculus heard the words inside his mind: *I'm not the boy you're looking for!*

Trioculus frowned again. "Don't try those Jedi mind games on me, Ken. Stronger Jedi than you have tried and failed. It won't work," he said with a sneer. And then he changed his sneer into a smile.

"Did you learn that trick in the Jedi Library, in the Lost City of the Jedi?" Trioculus asked.

Ken grabbed the bars of the cell and narrowed his eyes in a glare of anger. "Do you think I'll talk to *you*, Trioculus? You're a liar, a killer, and a destructive monster!"

"You flatter me," said Trioculus with an evil grin. "Which do you think I excel at the most? Lying? I'm indeed an expert at deception. Killing? No, every slave lord has to hold an execution now and then, it's only natural. But now tell me, why do you consider me a monster?"

"You burned the rain forests on the fourth moon of Yavin!"

"I had to do what I did to try to find the Lost City. So I could find you."

"Perhaps the Jedi Prince would like another candy-flavored bun," Tibor offered sarcastically, handing the boy a bun through the bars of his cell.

Ken's stomach was still groaning with hunger. He munched on the bun as the three-eyed Imperial ruler asked Tibor to depart, so he could talk to the prisoner alone, in private.

Tibor left as requested.

To foil spies and secret listening devices, Trioculus activated a small sound-wave scrambler he carried in his pocket. It would assure that no one else would hear what they were saying.

Ken yawned once more, feeling tired again. "Why did you want to find me?" Ken asked.

"Why, to become your protector, of course," Trioculus replied. "So you could leave the droids who raised you and be free."

Ken's eyelids felt weighted down, dragging him once again into sleep. What had Trioculus just said, he wondered? Things were becoming foggy. Uhmm—something about wanting to become Ken's protector . . .

"You—you don't care about me," Ken declared, struggling to remain awake. "You're a liar. I know why you've been looking for me. You want to destroy me because I know too much!"

"What do you think you know that I would care about?" Trioculus asked in a cagey tone.

"I know that you got to be ruler of the Empire by pretending you're Emperor Palpatine's son. But you're not. You're an impostor! I even know what you did to the Emperor's real son, Triclops. And that he's still alive!"

All three of Trioculus's eyes widened in alarm. "Such an imagination for a boy your age. You have a head full of absurd fantasies."

"You know I'm telling the truth. And if you try to hurt me, I'll escape and tell *everything* I know about you!"

"Who would you tell?" Trioculus asked.

"Kadann, the Supreme Prophet of the Dark Side," Ken said.

"Nothing escapes Kadann's attention," Trioculus said. "I sincerely doubt you could tell him anything he hasn't already foreseen in his prophecies."

"Then I'll tell all your enemies in the Empire! If they ever find out the truth about you, they'll assassinate you!"

Trioculus understood at once that this Jedi Prince *would* have to be destroyed, at any cost. If some of his enemies, who didn't know any better, were to find out the truth, they would begin a search for the Emperor's *real* son, and try to put that insane madman in power.

Trioculus had to stop that from happening. Palpatine's real son, Triclops, was too dangerous and destructive for even the Empire to tolerate. Trioculus and the Central Committee of Grand Moffs knew all too well that Triclops was incurably insane and a terrible threat. They had managed to imprison and hide him in Imperial insane asylums. But they knew it would be unwise to destroy him, because Triclops often betrayed himself. In his mad dreams, he had come up with many ideas that had proved useful to the Empire. His ideas—and inventions—had been essential to them for building certain weapons and machines of destruction.

"You're a young boy with strong opinions and dangerous ideas," Trioculus said, his voice suddenly becoming very gruff. "We shall meet again, Jedi Prince Ken. Very soon!"

Trioculus went back to see Zorba the Hutt at once.

"I want that boy," Trioculus said. "What is your price?"

Zorba gave a slobbering smile and chuckled. "I want just two things."

Trioculus clenched his fists. "Name them."

"Number one," said Zorba. "I want you to close down your factory barge here. Your smokestacks cause braze."

"A little braze never harmed anyone," Trioculus insisted.

"Hah!" Zorba exclaimed. "Hutts can't stand braze, and neither can tourists." Zorba wagged his fat tongue at Trioculus scoldingly. "Business in the casinos is down—*way* down—even though we're offering bigger jackpots than ever! Braze is driving our customers away—no one wants to come to Cloud City and breathe your foul smoke!"

"And the second thing?" said Trioculus, giving no hint of what his response would be to the first demand.

"Princess Leia. I know you have her. She murdered my son, Jabba, and she will pay with her life."

Trioculus knitted his eyebrows and frowned. "No. You cannot have Princess Leia."

Zorba pounded his right fist into his left palm. "Leia for Ken! One human traded for another! Fair is fair!"

"No," said Trioculus.

Zorba's pale, wrinkled face became inflamed, turning a bright, fiery red. "Yes!" Zorba hissed.

"No!" stormed Trioculus.

"Yes, yes, yes!! I am a Hutt, and a Hutt does not allow the murder of his son to go unavenged!" Zorba snorted, snarled, sneered, and then asked, "What use is the Rebel Alliance princess to you?"

"She will be my wife," Trioculus declared in a gruff, angry voice. "She will be Queen of the Empire!"

Hearing those words, Zorba's old heart nearly burst.

"And when she's my queen," Trioculus contin-

ued, "there will be new taxes on every casino in Cloud City, starting with your Holiday Towers. Taxes for Queen Leia. So she can have anything her heart desires!"

Zorba's yellow, reptilian eyes turned up in shock. He wheezed like a creature about to die.

"I want Ken," Trioculus repeated. "And for Ken I will give you . . . a new spaceship. They say the old *Zorba Express* is ready to be made into scrap."

Zorba spit on the ground near Trioculus's feet.

"Curse you, you three-eyed mutant!" he growled. "You will *never* get Ken!"

Trioculus leaned forward, turning his hands into fists. "Give me Ken, now! Or I will destroy Cloud City!"

Zorba's eyes narrowed and glowed like yellow fire.

"We met as friends today. We congratulated each other. But from now until the end of time, you and I are sworn enemies! And once a Hutt makes an enemy, there is no retreat until death!"

"It is you who will die for this, Zorba," Trioculus threatened.

"May I never look upon your ugly, scarred face again," Zorba replied.

Trioculus pressed a button on the communication device on his belt. Seconds later, the door to the penthouse was smashed to pieces as Trioculus's stormtroopers burst into the room, their blasters drawn.

But Zorba was just as fast on the button. His

signal summoned an attack team of Cloud Police, hiding just beneath the floor. As a trapdoor popped open, the room was suddenly swarming with Zorba's henchmen.

The sound of Zorba's belly laugh echoed throughout the room. "A-HAW-HAW-HAW!! . . ."

CHAPTER 8
Revenge at Last!

Zorba's penthouse was filled with blazing laserfire.

In the fast fury of combat, Zorba was struck several times, leaving small, black scorch marks on his thick, wrinkled skin. But his skin was tough enough to protect him. And he didn't stop laughing for even a second.

Zorba's twinkling yellow eyes watched with glee as his Cloud City Police devastated the stormtroopers using their new model laser pistols.

A few stormtroopers escaped from the penthouse suite with their lives. They fled down the hall and were captured by a second group of Zorba's Cloud Police, who were just arriving on the top floor to serve as reinforcements.

The moment he realized that his defense forces were being defeated, Trioculus, half-crazed by the maddening sound of Zorba's laughter, tried to escape too. But he ran smack into three approaching Cloud Police. They overpowered the three-eyed Imperial tyrant, shackled him, and took him directly back to the penthouse suite, to face Zorba the Hutt.

Zorba pointed to the Cloud Police. "Take him away. Take him to the room where we encase victims

in carbonite. I'll deal with him as soon as I return from destroying the factory barge—and Princess Leia along with it!"

While those momentous events were taking place in the penthouse suite, something almost as momentous was going on in the basement of the Holiday Towers Hotel and Casino.

A human guard brought a meal to Ken in his cell. But Ken was no longer hungry. He was now feeling much more alert, less tired, and able to make a plan of action.

Ken decided to try the Jedi mind trick he'd tried on Trioculus. But this time he would use it on the guard instead.

He concentrated. Freeing his mind of all thoughts except the thought of getting free, he imagined the guard's mind emptying—entering a state of total confusion.

"Can't you see that I'm not the boy you are looking for!" Ken exclaimed. "I'm Tibor, the bounty hunter! The prisoner tricked me and locked me in here! Help me get out of here, before he gets away!"

It worked! Thinking Ken was Tibor, the guard apologized and hurriedly unlocked the cell.

Soon Ken was outside the Holiday Towers building, running through the streets of Cloud City.

He passed many dazzling sights of the big city, including Masque Hall, where he peeked through a window to see the never-ending masquerade party.

Next he stumbled upon the Central Cloud Car Taxi

Port. Unfortunately his pockets were empty. He had no credits to pay for a ride back to Han Solo's sky house.

The Jedi mind trick had worked once, so Ken tried it again on the taxi driver. And once again it worked. Ken actually convinced the taxi driver that he had already paid for the ride!

On the Imperial factory barge, Luke and Kate were searching for Princess Leia.

Luke used the macrobinoculars he had brought with him to peer in the windows of every building he could see. He was trying to find any possible clue that might lead him to the princess.

Then at last, while staring at a room on the top floor of the tallest factory, he spotted her. She was smashing a window and crawling out onto a ledge. Luke looked higher with the macrobinoculars, checking out the roof of the building. There was a platform with a hovertransport. Around the corner of the building from Leia, he saw a service ladder that went up the side of the building—a ladder that could help them get up to her!

A short time later, when Luke met up with Leia on the ledge, she was so startled she almost fell, but then regained her balance.

"Leia! At last Kate and I found you!" Luke said. "There's a ladder to the roof around the corner. Quick—follow me!"

Leia, Luke, and Kate carefully climbed the ladder up to the flat, black roof. They scurried across it and soon reached the platform with the parked hovertransport.

Luke used the macrobinoculars again, this time to scan the brown sky above the tall smokestacks, looking to see if there were any Imperial vehicles flying nearby.

But instead of an Imperial vehicle he saw the *Millennium Falcon!*

Inside the *Millennium Falcon* Han Solo and Chewbacca were weaving in and out among the smokestacks, desperately searching for Luke, Leia, and Kate.

Laser cannons from the barge fired at the *Falcon* as Han descended low enough to spot the wrecked cloud car convertible. Then suddenly he heard a communication signal and a familiar-sounding voice!

"Millennium Falcon! Do you copy? Over."

It was Luke!

"I copy," Han said. "Where are you, Luke? Over."

"Check starboard, three-five. I'm piloting the Imperial hovertransport. This thing's a puddle jumper without even enough vertical thrust to get us home."

"I'll get below you and open the hatch," Han said. "Do you think Kate can make the jump into the *Falcon*? Over."

"Of course she can," Luke replied. "We're all ready to ditch this thing and fly back in style!"

In seconds the *Millennium Falcon* was flying directly below the hovertransport, a short leap away. Leia and Kate jumped out of the hovertransport first, falling safely into the *Falcon*. Then Luke set the hovertransport on automatic pilot and made the leap too.

Ground fire continued to target them. It missed the *Millennium Falcon*, but blew the hovertransport to pieces.

Luke looked around the cockpit of the *Falcon*. "Where's Ken?" he asked. "You didn't leave him home alone, did you?"

"Don't blame me," Han said, "but Ken got behind the wheel of my Custom Model-Q Foley and zoomed off for Cloud City."

"Han, he's just a kid!" Luke protested. "He's not even thirteen years old!"

"Tell that to him," Han said. "He seems to think he's old enough to drive in the Cloud Car Racing Finals. But don't worry, I sent Threepio, Artoo, and Chip to bring him back."

When Luke, Leia, and Kate were safely seated inside the *Millennium Falcon*, a fleet of very strange

looking spaceships appeared, each one a unique model from a different planet. There were dozens of them, and most of them were out-of-date models.

It was a fleet of bounty hunter spaceships. A ragtag fleet, the spaceships descended through the clouds until they were just above the factory barge.

Leading the pack was the ancient Huttian spaceship, the *Zorba Express*.

The *Millennium Falcon* soared away from the factory barge and over the Rethin Sea, just in time to avoid being spotted by the incoming fleet. From inside the *Falcon*, Han, Chewbacca, Luke, Leia, and Kate could see the fleet of spaceships attacking the factory barge.

The spaceships attacked relentlessly, dropping ion explosives, nova bombs, and doonium acid mines.

The entire factory barge began to quiver and tremble under the shock of the tremendous blasts.

At last Zorba the Hutt scored a direct hit on the central generator building—the domed power center for the Imperial barge.

In their last look back, Han, Chewbacca, Luke, Leia, and Kate saw the factory barge splitting in two and shattering.

A huge fireball rose into the plumes of brown smoke. Han Solo could practically feel the heat of the explosion behind him as the *Millennium Falcon* flew farther and farther away.

The factory buildings, smokestacks and all, plunged down into the sea of liquid rethin, then vanished as if they had never existed at all.

"A narrow escape, Chewie," Han said with a grin. "If I'd stopped for even half a minute to lubricate our subatomic accelerator, our friends here would still be down there, boiling in bubbling rethin."

Han wasn't the only one who was pleased with his timing. Zorba the Hutt was just as pleased, because he had information that Princess Leia was a prisoner in the tallest building on the barge, trapped in Trioculus's chambers.

And so he was convinced that Princess Leia had gone down with the factory barge, and that her mortal remains were now sinking deep into the liquid metal core of Bespin.

The death of Jabba the Hutt had been avenged! "A-HAW-HAW-HAW!! . . ." Zorba roared.

* * *

Zorba the Hutt returned directly to Cloud City, to the very room where Darth Vader once encased Han Solo in carbonite. There Trioculus was strapped to a hydraulic platform from which he could not escape.

"Your so-called Queen of the Empire is dead, Trioculus," Zorba announced. "Princess Leia's body is now sinking into the core of the planet, along with all your factories. So the next time a Hutt offers you a fair deal—a chance to trade one life for another—think twice before you refuse it." Zorba stroked his beard and wagged his thick tongue. "But I almost forgot. There won't *be* a next time for you. A-HAW-HAW-HAW . . ."

"You've sealed your doom, Zorba!" Trioculus shouted in defiance. "An armada of Imperial starships will come to destroy you—and Cloud City!"

Zorba thumped his massive tail on the floor in anger. "When the rumor gets out that you've been encased in carbonite and hidden somewhere in Cloud City, no Imperial will dare try to blow up this city. Besides, Cloud City was armed by the Rebel Alliance before I took it over from Lando Calrissian. We'll gladly defend ourselves against any stormtrooper invasion!"

"We can still make a deal, Zorba," Trioculus said. "I could share my power with you! You could become a grand admiral in the Empire!"

"Never," Zorba replied with a scowl. "I'd rather join the Rebel Alliance than raise the tip of my tail to help you! And now if you'll excuse me, I'm going to encase you in carbonite. Your body will be frozen and trapped, and your mind will be in constant torment!" Zorba licked his cheeks with his thick tongue. "Get ready . . . get set . . ."

"No, Zorba! Stop!"

"Go!!!" Zorba threw the switch, and the hydraulic platform was dropped into the pit.

"Ahhhhhhrrrrggghhh!" Trioculus screamed, the sound growing louder and louder.

In the pit there was bubbling liquid, gaseous fumes, and huge billows of smoke.

PZZZZZZT! SIZZZZZZZ!

The deed was finished.

Just as it had once been done to Han Solo, Trioculus's body was now trapped inside a block of carbonite.

Huge metal tongs then lifted the block out of the pit. Trioculus resembled a living sculpture; all three of his eyes now stared out in horror into the blackness in front of his face.

Soon Zorba broadcast his news from Cloud City, announcing the death of the Rebel Alliance Princess who murdered Jabba the Hutt! He warned all citizens to be alert for a possible Imperial attack, because Emperor Trioculus—now encased in a block of carbonite—was about to become a permanent, heavily guarded exhibit in the Cloud City Museum.

Inside the *Millennium Falcon,* they too heard Zorba's news broadcast.

"Trioculus has been carbonized—that's the best thing that's happened since I finished building my

sky house!" Han exclaimed. "But we've got to get you off the planet, Princess. If Zorba the Hutt finds out that you're still alive, sparks are going to fly. And I don't want you to be around when the trouble starts."

Making a quick stop at Han's sky house, they picked up Ken, along with Chip, Threepio, and Artoo-Detoo. The three droids had spotted Ken returning to Han's house in the cloud taxi. As Han packed up a few things, Ken frantically told everyone about his misadventures in Cloud City.

But they didn't hang around very long. For all Han knew, bounty hunters were spying on his sky house with macrobinoculars just to make sure that Leia was really dead.

As soon as they were all aboard the *Millennium Falcon*, Han set their course, punching codes into the navigation unit without giving anyone any clues about where he was taking them.

"You haven't even had a chance to enjoy your house yet, Han," Leia said. "I'm sorry you have to leave like this."

"Your safety comes first, Princess. For the time being, I'm leaving behind the life-style of a home-owner. I'm officially a traveling man again."

"Where should we go?" Luke asked the princess. "To the Rebel Alliance Senate on Yavin Four?"

"Too many Imperials between here and Yavin Four," Leia countered.

"If they board us for an inspection and find you," Han said, "Zorba the Hutt will be one of the first to hear the news."

"*Dweeeeboo Ptwaaa!*" Artoo tooted.

"Artoo suggests that perhaps we should head for your home planet, Han," Threepio translated. "The Corellian life-style has always been agreeable to droids."

"I've got another place in mind," Han replied.

"Where exactly?" Leia asked.

"Don't you like surprises?" Han asked.

"Is it a planet?" Ken added.

"Or is it a moon?" Luke asked. "Or an asteroid?"

"Or a space station?" Ken suggested.

"Let's just say it's a romantic place," Han said with a wink.

"Romantic, Han?" Princess Leia asked, smiling.

"Yes, Princess. Any objections?"

"None that I can think of," she replied. "As long as I have my brother along to chaperon," she teased. "Okay with you, Luke?"

"Affirmative," Luke replied. "Power up and engage sublightspeed thrusters!"

And they took off.

Han's sky house quickly became a speck of dust far behind them. Moments later, so did the planet Bespin.

"Luke, take over the accelerator for a minute, okay?" Han asked.

Luke took control of the acceleration lever and Han gave Princess Leia a kiss—a very long kiss.

While he was kissing Princess Leia, a crazy

thought popped into Han Solo's mind. Maybe he should propose marriage to her. Maybe it was about time that he popped the question.

But what would he say exactly? *Senator Leia Organa, could you ever love a mischievous Corellian pilot like me enough to say "I do" at the altar?* No—too stiff and formal. How about the simple approach? *Princess, will you marry me?* Nope. Too short, not enough affection. What about *Leia, will you be my wife and the mother of my children?* No, too old-fashioned.

It was a tough problem. A very tough problem indeed.

No doubt about it, he would have to wait until some other day to figure out how to say the words in just the right way. Or the day after some other day.

Ken smiled and gave Luke Skywalker a little nudge as they watched Han and Leia embrace. Luke waited until just after Han's and Leia's lips separated before pulling on the hyperdrive thruster, boosting their velocity far above light speed.

ZWOOOOOOSH! There was a blurry flash!

And then they were gone!

Glossary

Avabush spice
A spice that acts as a truth serum, also brings on sleepiness. Often it's baked into sweets, such as candy-flavored buns.

Bantha
A mammoth creature as large as an elephant, with tremendous looped horns. Ridden by Tusken Raiders as a form of transportation.

Bespin
The giant, gaseous planet where Cloud City is located. Bespin is located in the Bespin System. It has a core of liquid rethin metal, but its prosperity comes from the resources of its Tibanna gas mines. The Empire maintains a barge on Bespin that floats just above the Rethin Sea, with many factories for making war machines.

Braze
A word that is short for "brown haze," much as the word "smog" is short for "smoke and fog."

Carbonite
A substance made from Tibanna gas, plentiful on the planet Bespin, where it is mined and sold in liquid form

as a fuel in Cloud City. When carbonite is turned into a solid, it can be used for keeping humans or other organisms alive in a state of suspended animation, encasing them completely.

CB-99
A dusty, slightly bent, old barrel-shaped droid hidden in a secret room in the palace of Jabba the Hutt. He has a hologram file containing Jabba the Hutt's will.

Chip (short for Microchip)
Ken's personal droid, who lived with him in the Lost City of the Jedi and has now gone out into the world with him.

Cloud Police
The force that keeps the peace by enforcing the laws of Cloud City. Their leader is Chief Muskov, who does the bidding of the governor of Cloud City. The Cloud Police have a tradition of trying to remain neutral between the Alliance and the Empire.

Jabba the Hutt
A sluglike alien gangster and smuggler who owned a palace on Tatooine and consorted with alien bounty hunters. He was strangled to death by Princess Leia, choked by the chain that held her prisoner in his sail barge at the Great Pit of Carkoon.

Jawa
A meter-high creature who travels the deserts of Tatooine collecting and selling scrap. It has glowing orange eyes that peer out from under its hooded robe.

Jenet
An ugly, quarrelsome alien species. Scavengers, they have pale pink skin, red eyes, and sparse white fuzz that covers their thin bodies. They are sometimes known to hang out in the Mos Eisley Cantina.

Kate (short for KT-18)
A female, pearl-colored housekeeping droid that Luke buys from jawas on Tatooine as a housewarming gift for Han Solo.

Ken
A twelve-year-old Jedi Prince, who was raised by droids in the Lost City of the Jedi. He was brought to the underground city as a small child by a Jedi Knight in a brown robe. He knows nothing of his origins, but he does know many Imperial secrets, which he learned from studying the files of the master Jedi computer in the Jedi Library where he went to school. Long an admirer of Luke Skywalker, he has departed the Lost City and joined the Alliance.

Kip
The planet where Zorba the Hutt was kept prisoner for illegally mining gemstones.

Mos Eisley
A spaceport on Tatooine, made up of low concrete structures. The cantina at the spaceport is a dangerous place, a hangout for many outlaws and fugitives.

Ranats
Cunning and small, these powerful pests are ratlike aliens, with rodent tails and sharp teeth. They have now settled into Jabba's palace on Tatooine.

Repulsorlifts
Repulsorlifts keep Han's sky house, Trioculus's factory barge, and even Cloud City floating in the air.

Rethin Sea
The liquid metal core of the planet Bespin.

Sabacc
A popular casino card game in Cloud City.

Sandcrawler
A large transport used by the jawas.

Sky house
A new concept in dwellings, invented by Han Solo and Chewbacca, it is a house that uses repulsorlifts to float in the sky. Han owns the only sky house on Bespin. It floats on a cloud on the outskirts of Cloud City.

Tatooine
A desert planet with twin suns, Tatooine is Luke Skywalker's home planet.

Tibor
A bounty hunter who hangs out at Mos Eisley on Tatooine. Tibor is a Barabel alien—a vicious, bipedal reptiloid—

who has horny green scales. He is hired by Zorba the Hutt
to assist and serve Zorba in any way the Hutt desires.

Trioculus
Three-eyed mutant who was the Supreme slavelord of
Kessel. He is now Emperor. Trioculus is a liar and impostor who claims to be the son of Emperor Palpatine. In his
rise to power he was supported by the grand moffs, who
helped him find the glove of Darth Vader, an everlasting
symbol of evil.

Tusken Raiders
Also called sand people they live a nomadic life in some
of Tatooine's most desolate deserts. Often riding on
Banthas for transportation, they are vicious desert bandits
who fear little and make frequent raids on local settlers.

Twi'lek alien
A humanoid alien with a head tentacle, he is one of the
bounty hunters who hangs out in the Mos Eisley Cantina.

Zorba Express
Zorba the Hutt's ancient bell-shaped spaceship.

Zorba the Hutt
The father of Jabba the Hutt. He was unaware of his son's
death because he had been a prisoner on the planet Kip.
Zorba looks similar to Jabba, but he has long white braided
hair and a white beard. Jabba's will leaves all of his possessions to Zorba, including Jabba's palace, and the Holiday Towers Hotel and Casino at Cloud City on Bespin.

About the Authors

PAUL DAVIDS, a graduate of Princeton University and the American Film Institute Center for Advanced Film Studies, has had a lifelong love of science fiction. He was the executive producer of and cowrote the film *Roswell* for Showtime. *Roswell* starred Kyle MacLachlan and Martin Sheen and was nominated for a Golden Globe for Best TV Motion Picture of 1994.

Paul was the production coordinator and a writer for the television series *The Transformers.* He recently produced and directed a documentary feature entitled Timothy Leary's *Dead* and is currently directing a thriller about the space program. His first book, *The Fires of Pele: Mark Twain's Legendary Lost Journal,* was written with his wife, Hollace, with whom he also wrote the six Skylark Star Wars novels. The Davids live in Los Angeles.

HOLLACE DAVIDS is Vice President of Special Projects at Universal Pictures. Her job includes planning and coordinating all the studio's premieres and working on the Academy Awards campaigns. Hollace has an A.B. in psychology, *cum laude,* from Goucher College and an Ed.M. in counseling psychology from Boston University. After teaching children with learning disabilities, Hollace began her career in the entertainment business by working for the Los Angeles International Film Exposition. She then became a publicist at Columbia Pictures, and seven years later was named Vice President of Special Projects at Columbia. She has also worked for TriStar Pictures and Sony Pictures Entertainment.

Whether it's because they grew up in nearby hometowns (Hollace is from Silver Spring, Maryland, and Paul is from Bethesda) or because they share many interests, collaboration comes naturally to Paul and Hollace Davids—both in their writing and in raising a family. The Davids have a daughter, Jordan, and a son, Scott.

About the Illustrators

KARL KESEL was born in 1959 and raised in the small town of Victor, New York. He started reading comic books at the age of ten, while traveling cross-country with his family, and decided soon after he wanted to become a cartoonist. By the age of twenty-five, he landed a full-time job as an illustrator for DC Comics, working on such titles as *Superman, World's Finest, Newsboy Legion,* and *Hawk and Dove,* which he also cowrote. He was also one of the artists on *The Terminator* and *Indiana Jones* miniseries for Dark Horse Comics. Mr. Kesel lives and works with his wife, Barbara, in Milwaukie, Oregon.

DREW STRUZAN is a teacher, lecturer, and one of the most influential forces working in commercial art today. His strong visual sense and recognizable style have produced lasting pieces of art for advertising, the recording industry, and motion pictures. His paintings include the album covers for *Alice Cooper's Greatest Hits* and *Welcome to My Nightmare,* which was recently voted one of the one hundred classic album covers of all time by *Rolling Stone* magazine. He has also created the movie posters for Star Wars, *E.T. The Extra-Terrestrial,* the Back to the Future series, the Indiana Jones series, *An American Tale,* and *Hook.* Mr. Struzan lives and works in the California valley with his wife Cheryle. Their son, Christian, is continuing in the family tradition, working as an art director and illustrator.